Going Home Again

Going Home Again

Dennis Bock

Alfred A. Knopf · New York · 2013

THIS IS A BORZOI BOOK
PUBLISHED BY ALFRED A. KNOPF

Published in the United States by Alfred A. Knopf,
a division of Random House, Inc., New York.
Simultaneously published in Canada by HarperCollins Canada.
www.aaknopf.com

Library of Congress Cataloging-in-Publication Data

Bock, Dennis, [date]
Going home again / by Dennis Bock. — First edition
pages   cm
"This is a Borzoi book"—T.p. verso.
ISBN 978-1-4000-4463-4
1. Divorced men—Fiction. 2. Psychological fiction.
3. Domestic fiction. I. Title.
PR9199.3.B559G65 2013
813'.54—dc23   2012050903

Jacket image © Imagestopshop/Alamy
Jacket design by Chip Kidd

Manufactured in the United States of America
First Edition

first loves

*Move on, move on, as we are directed to do
at the scene of an accident, or a crime.*

—John Banville

Going Home Again

✈ Prologue

On the Friday evening before Kaj Adolfsson was killed, I was actually feeling pretty good about things. I had just landed in Madrid, which was home, and a big round sun the color of orange sherbet was three-quarters gone in a fine late-summer sky. I was coming off a strange year, a bit battered and bruised, but my circumstances were looking up. The language business was going well, my love life had crawled back up out of a deep dark hole, and the day after tomorrow I was hosting my daughter's thirteenth birthday. My problems seemed at that moment destined to disappear like that setting sun. And then, as I watched the city come into view from the backseat of my taxi, my brother's wife called with the news that set everything moving off in the wrong direction.

"And you haven't heard from him since?" I said, leaning forward and pointing to the dashboard radio. When the cabdriver reached for the dial to turn down the volume, I saw the little stub on his right hand where his index finger used to be.

"That's why I'm calling," Monica said. "I thought maybe he'd called you."

"No. Nothing. I just got in. There were no messages."

My brother and Monica were in the middle of a divorce full to overflowing with discord and grievance. Over the past year they'd told me in so many words that they each wished the other had never been born. Now she was on the phone telling me Nate's sailboat had been found crewless and adrift thirty miles south of Naples, Florida.

"The Coast Guard contacted me three hours ago. I don't know what to think. That stupid boat was his baby."

"*Is* his baby," I said, maybe a little too forcefully.

"He's two days overdue, Charlie. He was supposed to pick up the kids yesterday. Of course he doesn't show up. Now they call telling me his sailboat's under tow and do I know the whereabouts of my husband? The partners at his office haven't heard from him, either. No one knows a thing. You can imagine what this is doing to my head right now."

I did what I could to convince Monica that Nate was probably fine and all we could do was sit tight, he'd call soon enough. I'd be back in three days, on Monday, in any case. But after slipping the phone back into my pocket, I wondered if he wasn't already somewhere over the Atlantic en route to finishing up the business we'd left hanging between us. He was capable of much more than I could ever understand, that much I knew by then, and this sort of grand gesture—popping up in Madrid on the weekend of my daughter's thirteenth birthday—provided the retributive drama favored by a man on the verge of losing his family. I ran through as many likely explanations as occurred to me in the time it took to get into the city. But half an hour later, when the cabbie dropped me at the door of the Mesón Txistu, that feeling of unease still hung over me.

Men and women were sitting and standing in small groups taking aperitifs at the front bar when I walked in. I nodded to the bartender and continued up the stairs into the back room and found Isabel and Ava, our daughter, sitting at the table beneath the bull's head on the south wall, a pitcher of ice water between them. Ava's hair was shoulder length and chestnut brown, like her mother's, and she looked, despite my northern complexion, every bit the Spaniard. When she turned and saw me at the far end of the room, she got up and met me between tables, throwing herself into my arms. I gave her a spin and a hug.

"How was your flight, Daddy? How was *Ireland*?"

"It was good," I said, slipping out from under a shoulder strap. I handed her the lighter of two carry-on bags, the one loaded with presents. "You're looking great. How's Mom? She okay?"

"She's fine," she said, then led me by the hand to where Isabel sat, wearing a smile I wasn't quite able to pin down.

"Good to see you," I said, stooping to kiss both cheeks.

I didn't recognize the dress she was wearing that night. It was a green-and-white summery number that showed those great arms of hers, shaped and tanned at the tail end of an active and outdoorsy season. We'd been separated for more than a year now, and the fact that she had a man in her life was old news. Through a family friend named José, whom I'd known since my earliest days in Madrid, I'd heard more about him than I needed to know—for instance, that he was a constitutional lawyer in the Spanish Supreme Court and, at forty-two, the youngest justice in the history of the institution. He owned a house in Ibiza, as well as the flat in Paris I'd visited the previous Christmas. As far as I knew, he had no kids and lived the kind of life that stressed-out parents like to dream about.

The waiter appeared, helped me with my seat and left us with three leather-bound menus. Isabel was sitting directly across from me, Ava to my right.

"Are you feeling okay?" Isabel said. "You look worried."

"Just glad to be back," I told her. "No problem."

We usually spoke Spanish when the three of us were together. But for some reason we spoke English that night.

"You know Dad always looks tired, anyway," Ava said, opening her menu. "It's all that thinking he does. Right, Dad?"

"There you go," I said. "Nail on the head."

"I hope no one drops dead at my party," Ava said. "The heat's killed forty-one people in France this summer. Can you believe that?"

"That's horrible," I said.

"Mostly old people, I know. They were talking about it on the news this morning."

"At least it's cooler up there in the mountains," I said.

We'd celebrated Ava's birthday at a friend's house in the Madrid sierra, thirty-five minutes north of the city, for the past ten years. I'd flown into Dublin from Toronto that morning and spent the day putting out fires at the Bellerose Academy—one of the language schools I owned and operated—before hopping a shuttle over to Madrid for the occasion. Since splitting up the previous summer, her mother and I had managed to keep the lawyering to a minimum. Now, whenever we found ourselves in the same room together (which wasn't very often), we did our best to keep the edge out of our voices. In calmer moments we'd agreed that the success we'd have in raising our daughter would rise or fall in direct relation to the number of conflicting issues we chose to leave by the wayside. There just weren't enough hours in the day. Choose your battles. Wasn't that the best advice you could ever give or receive? By then it wasn't a question of solving anything or determining who was in the wrong, as too often someone was, but managing to move forward with our dignity intact.

"Grandpa's going to talk your ear off about his gardening. He's on this new thing. He's ordering papaya seeds from Brazil or something."

"And you?" I said, leaning forward to kiss her forehead. "What's up with you? I'm sure you've got a doozy waiting for me."

"Oh, yeah," she said, her big brown eyes glowing.

Ava liked to trot out riddles and tongue twisters and brainteasers as often as she could. I'd decided it was her way of focusing the mind on the solvable mysteries in life rather than dwelling on the incomprehensibles, like the annoying head-scratcher that her parents' marriage presented.

"This one will take you *at least* the weekend to figure out."

"Hold tight," I said, grabbing two corners of the table for emphasis.

"Okay, here goes," she said, looking at her mother, then me. "What's the difference between a *cat* and a *comma*?"

Isabel and I traded glances. We both put on an expression that showed our daughter we were really thinking.

"No idea," Isabel said.

"I can see a lot of ways they're different," I said, "but none of them is very clever."

"Wait. A cat and a *coma*?" Isabel said.

Ava swiped the air with an imaginary pencil. "Comma! *Comma!*"

"This one's a killer," I said.

"Just how I like them," she said.

"Good thing we have the whole weekend to stew over it."

A troubled look swallowed Ava's pretty smile when I said that. She began working her lips over the braces on her teeth. They still bothered her, I could see, though she wasn't much of a complainer about things like this.

"But we might not *last* through the whole weekend," she said. "What about that? People are dying all over Europe. Fifty people in France alone!"

"You just said it was forty-one," I told her.

"That was yesterday. By now it's fifty."

"What a tragedy," her mother said.

"You better not be giving up," Ava said. "Mom always says you give up too fast. In *every*thing."

Isabel's cheeks filled with color.

It was a characterization our daughter had heard often enough, I was sure. But I didn't bite. The waiter, now attending a table near ours, appraised us over half-moon glasses. Ava took a packet of sugar from a small cut-glass bowl in the centre of the table, ripped it open, poured it into her glass and began mixing it with a spoon. She sucked her lips over her braces again and then very sternly said, "A cat has its *claws* at the end of its *paws*. . . ." She put down the spoon, her face breaking into a smile. "And a comma is a *pause* at the end of a *clause*!" The air around her glowed.

"Very nice," I said. "The crown is yours."

She was the queen of riddles in the family and very smart indeed—in Spanish, English *and* French—even if she had hauled that brainteaser off some website. One day she was going to be a writer, she said, the next Simone de Beauvoir, Gloria Steinem and Naomi Wolf all wrapped up into one. Apparently (according to her mother) she was already talking about universities where she was interested in studying. For reasons unknown to me, there was one in Buenos Aires that figured at the top of her list. I had no idea what any of this was based on, though it heartened me to know that our daughter's possibilities were all the brighter for the fact that she was fluent in three languages.

Her Spanish mother spoke English well enough—quite well, in fact—but you needed a native speaker's proficiency to grasp a linguistic parallelogram as lovely as that. I asked Ava if she was going to translate for her mom.

"I would, but I'm sure you two have lots to talk about," she said. It was—and she knew it—the understatement of the year. She dipped a hand into the purse hanging on the back of her chair and produced one of those gargantuan novels she carried with her everywhere, opened it to where a green ribbon marked her place roughly halfway through, leaned forward and started reading.

Ava was our little scholar in the making. I'd always known she was a brilliant kid. But I was fully aware that a novel like that, in a situation like ours, was as much a shield against stupid adult high jinks and petty bickering as it was a rollicking good read. She was into something called dark fantasy at the time, which, if I understood correctly, usually included some sort of urban werewolf, a compulsive but sympathetic murderer or a vampire challenged by the crushing human need to be loved. I was sure that over the past year, since I'd left Madrid, she'd cast her mother and me in roles every bit as compromising and bloody as those she chose to read about. I'd never asked her how those novels typically ended, whether in bloodbath or in reconciliation, or which of the two endings, the gory or the romantic, she preferred; but I knew—and not without the guilt that still kept me awake at night— she hadn't given up on us yet.

Thirteen years on and I could still remember clearly the weeks leading up to the day Ava was born: the rolling waves of anxiety and excitement; how Isabel walked around with her right hand pasted to the side of her amazingly huge stomach; the endless baths she ran, blue candles placed around the edge of the tub. And at night how the mysterious being inside her pressed itself against my waiting hand, like she was already fully conscious in there and just counting down the days. And when I finally held our daughter in my arms for the first time, I felt that she'd been part of me my whole life. The feeling was so powerful I found myself moved to tears.

The fact that Ava was turning thirteen probably made a bigger impression on me than it made on her. It almost felt that night as if I were stepping into a finished painting, and all I had to do to figure out what that painting meant was get to the other side of this weekend. Ava was excited, of course—she was the one getting the presents and blowing out the candles. But my first year as a bachelor in two decades was just coming to a close, and now like magic, as if time had snapped its fingers, it came to me that I was in the middle of a life I hadn't really paid much attention to. My old self was buried in the irretrievable past, the world had continued, and suddenly my baby daughter was a teenager.

"And your brother?" Isabel said.

Going Home Again

I glanced at Ava to make sure she was deep into her book. "Difficult, as usual," I said. "Bit of a prick, actually."

"Don't tell me he's the same," she said.

"Worse."

And like a spy in one of those old movies, Ava lowered her book conspicuously, stared at us for a moment, then slipped back into her story.

⇥ One

There was no reason
to think anything would be different between me and
my brother the previous summer, in 2005, when I
called ahead to tell him I was coming back to Toronto
to try out my new life as a single man. I'd been studying
the possibility of taking the business across the Atlantic for years, but for too many reasons to count, I'd
never managed to pull it off. After finding out about
the Supreme Court justice named Pablo, though, and
having by then bunkered down at the Reina Victoria Hotel for two months, I was feeling sufficiently
unsettled to actually do it. I needed some changes in
my life. New schedule, new people, new rhythms. I
was hoping for something else but wasn't at all sure
what it might be. The challenge of setting up my fifth
language academy was a project that would focus my
energies in the meantime and perhaps turn off the
panicked voice in my head that kept telling me things
I didn't want to hear.

I wondered if some overlooked germ of hope had
lain dormant in my heart over the years since I'd last
seen my brother. But it wasn't an easy telephone call
to make at the time. There had always been some fundamental confusion between us, a wall, in effect an

unending failure to imagine how the other saw and thought about the world that too often made things go sideways between us. That's what had happened in Madrid the last time I'd seen him. We'd spoken by phone half a dozen times since then—on a birthday, his or mine, or the shared anniversary of our parents' deaths—and I'd always come away glad to know he was well but also relieved that our lives were separate and distinct and that the problems between us might remain buried to the end of our days.

They had met only once, Isabel and Nate, when he came through Madrid back in 1992, the summer of the Barcelona Olympics and the Seville World's Fair, after dumping the girl he was traveling with in France. He turned up at our door one night and told us he was heading down to check out the señoritas in Seville, then going back north to try to score some tickets for the sailing competitions in Catalonia. We put him up on the couch for a week. Showing him around my adopted hometown, I took him to the oldest restaurant in the world and spent a wad of money I didn't really have. We wandered through neighborhoods packed with bars and clubs. Nothing seemed to impress him. In fact he found it all just a little bit irritating. The city was too hot and dirty and loud; he bitched and moaned about train schedules and shitty restaurants and the near-complete absence of spoken English in the streets and hotels. I got the impression that every-thing he saw in Spain made him feel superior, though of course he didn't say as much. His last night with us he got stupidly drunk and said he wanted to go find some prostitutes. At first it was a joke I could almost brush aside. But he kept insisting. Then he draped his arm around Isabel's neck and asked if out of the goodness of her heart she could possibly loosen that grip she'd fastened around my balls, the boys just wanted to go out and have some fun for a change. That's when I took him out for a drink he didn't need and told him he could find some other couch to sleep on. I knew he had some experience with prostitutes. I didn't care so much about that, since we both did. What I couldn't stand was him treating Isabel as if she were some sort of obstacle in my life. The whole week had been building up to that moment. He'd been throwing out little put-downs and challenges, testing to see how far he could push me. When I told him what a selfish prick I thought he was, he took a swing at me right there in front of the bar. Not nearly as drunk as he was, I just stepped aside, went back to the apartment and took Isabel out to dinner. His backpack was gone when we got home a few hours later. The taps in the kitchen and bathroom were open full blast and a jug of water had been emptied into our bed. It was probably three or four years before I talked to him again.

So I was surprised, maybe even a little suspicious, I'll admit now, when he offered to pick me up at the airport. What might have changed, I wondered. A few hours into my flight I became convinced it had to be a misunderstanding and doubted he'd show. At baggage collection I watched an empty baby bassinet make three solitary revolutions and weighed my immediate prospects. I had a pocketful of euro coins that weren't going to do me a lick of good here, a cell phone with thirty-seven Madrid numbers on speed dial and one single solitary local address written out on an old Post-it in my wallet. For an uncomfortable moment I felt something like a college student on the first leg of the big trip, tired, woefully underprepared and full of conflicting emotion. I saw my brother for an instant then—he was standing in the concourse—when the automatic doors that separated us opened. I almost didn't recognize him, not because he'd changed—he hadn't—but for the simple shock of seeing him there.

He was holding a newspaper in his right hand and wearing jeans and a green golf shirt. I might have smiled when I saw him—surprised he'd actually come to meet me—and then I wondered if he somehow knew I was limping home at the end of my marriage. Would he remind me, after thirteen years apart, that he'd always come out on top in the competition that seemed to rule us? Steeling myself, I collected my luggage and continued to the doors. He saw me and waved, and when we embraced, I recognized the cologne that our father had worn when we were boys. I didn't know what it was called, but its scent opened my eyes like an old family photograph.

"My big little brother," he said. "Welcome home."

"It's good to see you, Nate," I said.

I'm taller than my brother by two fingers, have been since I caught up and passed him at the age of fourteen, and when we stood back from our embrace,

he put his hand on my shoulder—the railing still separated us at hip level—and nodded and smiled as if some
pleasant observation was registering in his mind. His
hair was thick and dark, gelled or greased and cut short
in a way that made him look younger than his years.
He looked more or less as I remembered him. He was
a fit and handsome man, like our father, with strong
shoulders and a natural athletic grace that had favored
him throughout and beyond his high school years. I
couldn't begin to imagine how much my appearance
had changed since then. I had expected a similar aging
in my brother, of course, the beginnings of a paunch
or the thinning of hair that followed on our father's
side. But there was no hint of that. The years seemed
to have passed him by. His face was still unlined and
youthful-looking, his dark hair was thick as ever, and
he wore the same conspiratorial and dazzling smile
he'd used to his advantage when we were kids.

There were no awkward silences between us that
day. As he drove me into the city—we were riding in
air-conditioned comfort in a big white Escalade that
afforded us a bird's-eye view of the laps of the drivers
in the next lane—he mentioned his kids three or four
times, how great they were, what they did for fun, how
he liked nothing more than hanging out in the backyard and grilling hot dogs and burgers for them. Sticking to the upside of my life, I told him that Ava was
an athletic and popular kid, almost twelve years old at
that point, a kid who loved to read, did great in school
and had a knack for languages. "Can you believe it? Us
as dads," he said. "The mind boggles."

A few minutes later he pointed out an office tower in the distance, tall and glassy and shimmering in the afternoon sunshine, sixty stories of gold-tinted windows. He was a partner with one of the big law firms in that building, specializing in sports and entertainment. His client list had a number of golf and baseball and hockey players on it. The only name that stood out for me was a young female tennis player's, likely because I'd always kept an eye on that game for its connection to memories of summer evenings spent rallying tennis balls against the south wall of my high school. Cycling, tennis and swimming had been my areas of concentration, solitary sports whose lack of bullish camaraderie seemed to make him suspicious at the time.

"Sounds like you enjoy what you do," I said. "There aren't a lot of guys around these days who can make that claim."

"I'm not saying life's perfect where I'm sitting. I've got a bit of a domestic situation going on."

"Oh?"

He told me that Monica—his sons' mother—had moved out in April, three days after tossing her wedding band into the Toronto harbor at the end of a night on the town with three girlfriends. Now she was living with an older Swedish man who owned what he described as a multidimensional sports-and-entertainment complex for the modern adventure-seeking kid, a high-end, one-stop birthday emporium called Wonderworld. The man in question had come over from Scandinavia in the early nineties and doggedly built a chain of these franchises across the country.

"That's where she met the guy. At our kid's tenth birthday party. Nice, eh?"

"I'm sorry to hear it," I said.

Since then Nate and Monica had hashed out an agreement where the kids were concerned. Everything else was still up in the air. Technically he took his sons every other week, but now he was traveling so much and so often that he was barely able to keep up his end of the deal. His tone when he told me this wasn't whiny or bitter, not on that first afternoon, anyway. If anything he seemed contemplative—a word I never expected to use to describe my brother. But that's how he came off that day as he drove me into the city. It seemed he'd been humbled. It stood to reason. You can't go through something like that and not be.

I listened to the rest of his story, then told him something of my own great humbling. The two stories were dishearteningly similar.

He nodded in agreement. "Yeah," he said, "that sounds just about right. Bang, bang, bang. Half the marriages on our street have gone bust. It's a freaking epidemic here. Maybe it's different in those Catholic countries. But here . . ." He shook his head again, then smiled.

"What?"

"You know those little fridge magnets? The ones with writing on them? Some little bead of wisdom or saying or whatever to warm your day."

"Sure. I think so."

"We had one on our fridge forever. I didn't think much about it. I thought it was just a joke. It used to give me a laugh."

"What did it say?"

"'Men are like floors. If you lay them right the first time, you can walk all over them for years.'" He smiled a big genuine smile.

"Who's going to argue with that, right?" I said.

"But that was her basic philosophy. Typical passive-aggressive bullshit that women get away with all the time now. Maybe it's different over in Spain, who knows? But a guy puts some sexist joke about women on his fridge here, he's automatically a misogynist and creepy asshole. Stay long enough, you'll see for yourself."

Nate lived in the city's east end, two blocks north of the old Don Jail, in a nice-looking neighborhood set at the edge of a deep, wide valley. When he led me through his house that afternoon he told me it had been featured in *House & Home* and *Architectural Digest;* he managed to impart this information without seeming to brag, though of course that's exactly what he was doing. He directed my attention to an oversize book on the coffee table called *Rustic Cottage Ontario,* and when he flipped it open to a photograph showing the vacation property he'd recently bought two hours north of the city, I told him it looked like things were going well for him.

And it was true. The walls in the room he'd led me into were hung with colorful paintings, and the hardwood floors were covered in fine rugs. The overall feel of the place was original, homey and expensive. It seemed he'd made himself into a success. But I hadn't intended the comment to be understood this way, if in fact it had been. I'd meant to say that he'd taken his life in a positive direction, or so it appeared, given what the details seemed to suggest. Despite the domestic situation he'd referred to, my brother had ended up a family man, or at least some version of one. I saw the traces everywhere: a golf putter, a baseball glove, a heavily thumbed copy of the latest *Harry Potter;* playing cards were scattered over the dining room table; a Monopoly set was open midgame on the coffee table beside the cottage book. Someone had left a skateboard in the middle of the living room floor, and rather than cursing and stepping over it as we moved into the kitchen he lowered his foot decisively against its stern, and the board obediently popped up into his hand, and he tucked it under his arm with a smile. It was a trick he might have performed in the family driveway thirty-five years before. And that's when I wondered for the first time if my brother had truly changed. Had I judged him too harshly? Had I even remembered him correctly after all those years?

Two cats appeared from behind a couch, one black, one white, and disappeared up the carpeted stairs. He leaned the skateboard against the wall, its wheels still spinning noiselessly, and grabbed two bottles of Heineken from the fridge. We stepped out into the backyard. Overhead was the sort of sky that seems to go on forever. There was nothing but blue up there and a single widening and blurred contrail that cleaved the heavens in perfect halves. "To the end of long journeys," he said, raising his bottle. The small tree fort that sat in the crotch of an old maple at the far end of the garden was awash in afternoon sunlight. The fort was painted a cheerful Mediterranean blue that held the light with a sharp warm glow, and the driftwood and cedar trees that bordered the property seemed to lean inward, as if they were expectant of some rivalry that might now make itself known and listening intently.

"This is your place now. For as long as you want. Seriously. We set up a room upstairs."

I told him I appreciated the offer, that it meant a lot to me, but I'd booked a room in a hotel downtown.

He insisted, shaking his head. "That's not how it works here," he said. "You're our guest. Absolutely not. No way. You're not leaving. The boys have been looking forward to this. They've heard all about Uncle Charlie now. You can't just suddenly disappear. They've been talking nonstop about—" And with this he smiled and gestured over my shoulder. I turned and there were his sons, Titus and Quinn, big grins eating up their faces. They were both wearing baseball caps and long, brightly colored shorts. "Thing One and Thing Two," he said.

Titus was ten that summer, two years younger than Ava, but he was already as tall. His head came up to my chin. I shook hands with both boys. They were perfect little gentlemen that afternoon.

"Welcome to Canada," Titus said. "It's very nice to meet you." With his thick curly brown hair, he looked much like I did at that age. He was gangly and awkward, at the point in a boy's life where muscle and coordination seem to disappear under the blitzkrieg of skeletal growth. Quinn, two years younger, was blond and cheerful as a brand-new sports shirt.

Both boys' eyes were brown, like their dad's, Ava's, and our father's. Well tanned and radiantly healthy, they'd just finished two weeks of canoe day camp on the Toronto Islands. They told me what sports and hobbies they'd done there, and I pulled out some pictures of their cousin and told them that she loved swimming and playing soccer, too, and that with any luck one day they'd meet.

"But why does she live over there?" Quinn said.

"That's where she's from, you idiot," Titus said. "She's *Spanish!*"

"But Uncle Charlie's not Spanish, are you?" Quinn said.

"I'm from here. Just like your dad. I went away for a long time. And now, *poof,* I'm back."

Titus seemed to take this as a satisfactory explanation and then, apropos of nothing I was aware of, showed me what he'd learned in karate class earlier that week. He waved his little arms in the air and did a few turns and kicks, ending with a horizontal chop.

Quinn looked at me and rolled his eyes. "Okay, ninja boy," he said.

Nate slipped inside and returned with another round for us and a bag of Oreos for his kids. "If this isn't a special occasion," he said, tossing the bag to Titus, "I don't know what is."

I canceled my room at the Marriott and stayed with Nate and his sons for a week until my rental was available. Things went fine those first few days.

We played sports and toured around the neighborhood during the day, and when Nate got home just after seven, he joined us in the backyard, two bottles of Heineken in hand, and threw some steaks or burgers on the barbecue and put together a salad.

We'd end up spending most of the night out there, talking and drinking and reminiscing, the boys listening to our stories. As the evening light softened and slipped away altogether, the sound of music and voices in one or another of the adjoining properties rose up through the trees and played on as a colorful backdrop to our memories. Titus and Quinn would get bored around then and drift up to the family room to turn on the TV. But we stayed out there long into the night catching up, talking about our lives and relationships and how much our kids meant to us, and I felt for the first time in years that my brother and I were able to talk about things that were important to us without getting tangled up in the weeds.

That I began to like my brother again couldn't have surprised me more. He'd turned into a pleasant man. The last sorry image I had of him—stumbling over that wild punch on the sidewalk outside a Madrid bar—began to fade. If the shadows were just right, I could see our father's face in the silhouette against the porch light above the sliding back door. I wondered if I'd been misjudging him all along. We talked about his first love, sailing, and his sons' soccer and hockey skills, how he and I needed to keep our kids insulated from the troubles that plagued divorcing parents. One night I showed him all the pictures I had of Ava. Smiling and nodding, he seemed to give each one a good measure of his attention. "She's going to break hearts one day," he said.

"Mine, at least. That's for sure."

On the third or fourth day the boys took me to a public pool just a few minutes from their house. The day was already hotter than it needed to be, and I was feeling up for a bit of exercise and sunshine. After Nate left—he was driving down to Detroit that morning— we got into our bathing suits and walked over. The teenager at the front desk of the grey cinder-block building you needed to pass through to get to the pool checked us in and handed over the color-coded wristbands everyone under the age of twelve had to wear. We walked through the men's changing room and down a slippery tiled corridor that led us through the building to the fenced-in pool on the other side. The water and decks were crowded with pink and red and black bodies splashing around or lying out in the sun. We found an empty patch of cement, dropped our towels and got in the pool.

After a few minutes I pulled up to the edge and

watched the city of glass towers on the far side of the valley come to its full morning expression of shimmering light. In my years away I'd sometimes glimpsed the city on a TV screen or in a magazine article. Once, I saw it on the cover of a brochure at a travel agency in Madrid while shopping for plane tickets to Prague. It stood for the place I had yearned to run away from, the place I'd lost, and it had the charming and minor-key bravado of a city that still seemed too much in search of itself and at the same time too inclined to declare itself as one to be reckoned with. For me, it was a hometown by default and cruel luck, since Nate and I came here to live with our uncle after our parents were killed in a car crash. I'd attended high school and bided my time until I was old enough to jump ship. I appreciate now how little I thought about Toronto all the years I lived in Madrid. But on those rare occasions when I was reminded of it, when a memory or emotion surfaced, it stayed with me for an hour or a day until my regular life took over again.

It was close to noon when a man dressed in the staff uniform approached the side of the pool and pointed into the crowd of swimmers. He was roughly my age, maybe a few years older. In his right hand a bullhorn was lowered at his side. A silver whistle and a bunch of keys on a string hung from his neck. Beside him stood a woman holding the hand of a girl who looked to be nine or ten years old. The woman, about forty, wore dark bug-eyed sunglasses and was dressed in an orange one-piece. She pointed to the middle of the shallow end. The movement and splashing in this area stopped and slowly the swimmers parted around Titus. He raised himself to a standing position and walked toward the man, who was beckoning him to come over. I lowered myself into the water and crossed to the opposite side.

"What's going on here?" I said.

Titus shrugged, hands pressed flat against the concrete deck. "No idea," he said.

"Are you this boy's father?" the man said.

I identified myself as his uncle and asked again what was going on.

"Both of you please remove yourselves from the pool and come with me," he said.

As if to protect her daughter, the woman placed her hand over the girl's shoulder when I lifted myself out of the pool, and they marched off alongside the man, Titus, Quinn and I following behind, my arm around Titus's shoulder, to a glass-walled office that gave onto the pool.

"You're sure this is the boy?" the man asked the woman as he positioned himself on the opposite side of a large desk, and she nodded. When I saw Quinn standing out on the deck, staring in at us from the other side of the glass door, I gave him a wink, and he smiled and rolled his shoulders with a questioning shrug. In the pool behind him the circle that had widened around his brother filled again with swimmers.

The girl wore a green two-piece bathing suit and a thin silver necklace. Her long blond hair was wet and pressed against the side of her head in curling thick cords, and goose bumps pocked her arms and legs. She was standing beside her mother, as far from me and Titus as the small room would allow.

"Maybe this was an accident?" the man said, hopefully, I thought, his eyes moving slowly between me and the woman. "You think that's possible? It's a crowded pool right now. Look at it out there. This sort of thing can happen."

"I'm sorry," I said, "but what are we talking about here?"

"The girl has told her mother that this boy—your nephew—touched her body. Very directly. She referred specifically to a certain part of her body. And that it happened more than once."

"Two times," the woman said.

Titus didn't raise his eyes to mine when I looked at him. "Do you know what he's talking about?" I said.

"No," Titus said.

"Are you sure you understand what's being said here?" I saw the first trembling take his upper lip when I laid my hand on his shoulder.

"I didn't do anything like that," he said.

"You're sure that didn't happen?"

"I didn't touch anyone like that. Quinn and I were playing. We were just swimming. I didn't even notice her."

"You know this is for real, right?" I said. "Is what you're saying the truth?"

"Yes," he said, looking up at me. "It's the truth."

"Okay, buddy. Go wait outside with your brother."

Once he was standing out there on the deck a

moment later, his small shoulders began to quake and roll with sobbing.

"You should be ashamed of yourself," I said, turning to the woman. "Look what you've done to that poor kid."

"That's an ignorant statement considering the circumstances," she said. An unpleasant distortion of her pretty daughter's, her little carnivorous mouth turned narrow and sharp.

"He brushed up against your daughter in a crowded pool. There's a hundred people in there."

"I am protecting my daughter," she said. "That's my job. I am her mother."

"God knows with a mother like you I can see why she's got fear in her heart."

Her face, already distorted with anger, seemed to change shape altogether. "I want this man and those children removed from here," she said, turning to the supervisor.

"I'll have to ask you to leave, sir. I'm very sorry."

"Did it occur to you that the boy might be telling the truth?" I said. "Did it occur to you that the only reason this woman's got the upper hand here is because she's the one who's going to start shouting? Is that how it works here? The loudest one wins?"

"This is a difficult situation," the man said. "If you could understand my position."

"I'm not sure your position has anything to do with it," I said.

"That boy should be on some sort of registry,"

the woman said. "He should be identified and put on some sort of registry. Parks and Recreation should know about people like him. Who knows how many girls he's done this to."

"He's ten years old!"

"That's the scary part," she said wildly, as if vindicated.

"What's scary is people like you destroying a perfectly innocent afternoon."

"This afternoon is far from innocent, thanks to you."

"And when something bad *does* happen, what then?" I said. "You won't even know enough to recognize it. And neither will your daughter because she's been so warped by you."

"Are you *threatening* us?" she said, pulling the girl tight against her.

"Oh, for Christ's sake," I said. "You're so completely—"

The man stepped out from behind his desk, his whistles chiming merrily.

"Forget it," I said. "Don't bother. We're done here."

I slammed the door on the way out. We collected our towels and flip-flops and steered toward the exit.

"What's going on?" Quinn said. "What did he do?"

"Nothing," I said. "Some people are just idiots."

That walk seemed to last forever. The corridor echoed with voices and the sounds of locker doors creaking and slamming. We finally emerged on the other side, walked past the teenager handing out the wristbands and stepped out into the bright day.

Whether the incident had been big enough to merit a larger conversation or simply left behind I couldn't be sure. Titus had cried, briefly, but seemed fine once we got out of there. One afternoon at the Retiro Park in Madrid something similar had happened to me and Ava. I remembered that now as we walked back into our afternoon. Ava and I had been strolling on a path on a fine spring day when we approached a man lying on the grass with his hand tucked under a heavy coat. I turned Ava in the opposite direction—she was probably seven at the time—before she noticed anything. Nothing happened. We continued our walk, found an open-air café and ordered hazelnut milk shakes. But for days afterward I wondered if I'd done the right thing—turning away from the situation, rather than shaming the man or siccing the police on him.

I didn't tell Nate about the woman at the pool when we sat up later that night talking about the baseball season and the bench-clearing brawl that happened earlier that day at Comerica Park in Detroit. He'd been sitting behind home plate when Runelvys Hernández picked off Carlos Guillén with a bullet pitch to the head. It was a hell of a fastball, he said, and an intentional attack, no doubt about it. We had drinks and a couple of serious Cohibas going. He told the whole story like an old pro recounting the good old days, sitting there rolling that cigar between his fingers or dusting off the ash against the bottom of his sandal. The crickets were humming away out there in the dark. The kids were upstairs watching a movie, and it was like one of those summer nights I remembered from when we were kids and it seemed that our neighborhood had little or no connection to the world as we knew it in the daytime, as if the dark were a knife that split open the world to show us another dimension entirely.

Monica came by the house to collect the boys in the morning. I was in the kitchen eating a bowl of cereal and going through the listings a real-estate agent had sent over. I'd started looking for a space for the new academy by then. Nate was sitting at the kitchen table reading the newspaper. When the doorbell rang, I saw the sad look of resignation descend over his face. Slowly he closed the paper, got up and went to let her in.

I heard only a tinge of impatience and tension when a female voice said, "But I'd like to *meet* him, if you don't mind."

A strained silence followed, and the clearing of a throat, then the sound of a heel turning on the polished floor. Upstairs, a heavy rapid thumping began, as if one of the boys had started performing ollies on a skateboard up there in the hallway.

An athletic-looking woman, blond and broad-shouldered, Monica was exactly the sort of girl my brother used to date in high school. We shook hands in the hallway by the stairs after Nate went up to hurry the kids along. She was wearing faded jeans, a baseball cap, a red blouse and sandals. I knew she worked as a producer on a live call-in sports show called *The Sports*

Animal and, since moving in with the Swedish businessman, had started training for a marathon.

"The boys can't stop talking about you," she said, her wide, pleasant mouth breaking into a Julia Roberts smile.

"They're great kids. I'm glad I've finally met them."

It was easy to see her younger son's dark eyes in hers. I didn't know what else to say. Here was the woman who'd stabbed my brother in the heart. At that moment I felt for him as deeply as I did for myself. We'd been dealt the same hand and now were obliged to grit our teeth and move on. Upstairs I heard the impatient bass of my brother's stressed-out voice telling Titus and Quinn to get ready for the transfer.

"I wanted to say thank you," she said. We were in the kitchen now, standing in the light streaming through the glass doors.

"For what?" I said.

"What you did at the pool. Titus called and told me what happened."

"That woman was a nut. Don't mention it."

"He said you stuck up for him. That means a lot to me."

"You're welcome. I felt terrible for him."

Once they'd cleared out, Nate gave me a long, hard stare. "What do you think about that?"

"It's tough," I said.

"You're telling me. Six months ago we're talking about the Mayan Riviera. It almost feels like a sick joke. Sometimes I think I'd like to stick a fork in her eye."

I didn't know the half of what had gone on between

them, but I was prepared and even inclined to take his side. All I knew was that she'd taken a lover, and that was enough for me. She had moved from one bed to another in the space of two or three days. Despite all I knew about my brother's failings, this fact in my eyes was resonant enough to absolve him of all sins. I didn't mention this as I listened to him rhyme off his list of complaints about Monica and the general injustice he'd been dealt, but his kids had looked happy to be transferring over to their mother. When they'd finally come downstairs with their little backpacks crammed to overflowing with books and clothes, they'd hung off her in a way that had caused a hopeful note to ring somewhere at the top of my heart. They would be fine with her. It had also caused me to wonder about my own situation with Ava. If the boys were pleased to go off with their mother at that point, wouldn't my daughter, if pushed, likely follow the same pattern? She would go—in fact had gone—with her mother on countless occasions rather than riding it out with the old man. I didn't draw this question of loyalty to my brother's attention. He was as aware of it as I was, and another kick in the balls wasn't something he needed right then. What he needed to do was vent, to cast Monica as the villain. It was his right to do so. How could you find fault in a man's anger after such a wounding? I did everything a brother can do at a time like that. I shut up and listened and nodded my head and agreed with him in spirit that she was a lousy human being who could stand to learn a thing or two about common decency and respect.

That afternoon I turned his situation around in my head. What came to mind was the realization that our loved ones were capable of far more than we were able to handle. Wasn't that a lesson we could take to the bank—that there were conflicting worlds within us all, and those worlds were ready and willing to defy us at the worst possible moment? As was my own, my brother's life was proof enough of this. There was no reason to feel surprise that the woman who'd wounded him so deeply had seemed a decent person when we'd spoken—a decent person who'd happened to destroy my brother's family and then been able to thank me with real sincerity for sticking up for her son—and that it was likely that Nate, suddenly poleaxed and humiliated, was the only person alive who felt as he did about her, which was angry and resentful as hell.

We took the boys to Toronto's annual book festival the third weekend of September. I'd moved into my rental by then, a nice three-bedroom semidetached house, and was more or less settled in, physically, anyway; and the office space, under lease now for a five-year term, was in the middle of renovations. There was a fresh bite of autumn in the air, and the sky was clear and wide and blue. It was a rare day. I was feeling the same sort of optimism I recalled experiencing at the start of a new school year, when everything seemed possible, and expectation and promise and goodwill swelled in your heart.

The festival was staged in the park between the

Royal Ontario Museum and the pink-granite edifice of our provincial Parliament buildings. Under the wide canopy and random patches of blue sky, we trolled the booths and kiosks, thumbing through magazines and books. It was carnival, county fair and trade show pinned like a butterfly under a bright autumn sky.

I hadn't told Titus that the author of the novels I'd seen him reading and rereading around the house would be signing his books here today. The writer in question was scheduled to give a presentation midafternoon. What this might entail I had no clue, but the advertisement had called it a "signing event," and I was hopeful that Titus would be pleased. The three-volume series was in the backpack I was carrying, and now, twenty minutes before the event would begin, we snacked on hot dogs at a picnic table under a big maple. I was watching people flowing past, taken by the simplicity of the moment and the warm sun on my face, when in the crowd I saw the woman I'd dated and lived with back in my university days. Her name was Holly Grey, and she had been my first love.

It was very clearly her. I knew this with absolute certainty, though people passed between us and her back was partially turned. It helped, I suppose, that she'd neither gained nor lost any weight, and her hair was much the same, despite being cut shorter now than I remembered it. I was suddenly in another time and place. And then after an instant I was back again.

She was wearing a long grey skirt, a light blue blouse and a leather-strap necklace that looped three or four times around her neck. She looked elegant and graceful and beautiful. In fact she looked better than she had at twenty-three. I saw her hands moving with that casual familiarity I remembered, and when she turned her head slightly, I caught the smile at the corner of her mouth.

She was standing in line with a young man at the roti and shawarma stand, close enough that I could have called out to her if I'd wanted to. Holly seemed, I didn't know what—happy? Animated? Pleased with the world? At that moment I was a man gazing into the deepest pool of them all, that of the irretrievable past, and trying to figure out his part in it. I could see only Holly's back and arms and hands, which were moving as gracefully as if she were illustrating a story for the benefit of the young man she was standing with. I remembered that about her. She was animated. Once, she'd scratched her forearm so hard with a fingernail—making some point I don't recall—that she actually drew blood. I can't say I was moved to jealousy or regret when I saw her now, though a powerful nostalgia took root in my heart. It was an odd stirring that startled me, some combination of puzzlement, awe and whimsy.

She turned as the music began. I hadn't noticed the silence, but when the heavy steel drums started somewhere behind us, the clamor filled the park as if a new light had been thrown down from the sun, and the world felt cheery and bright. It was an African or Caribbean lineup, and the six or seven individuals, dressed in yellow and white and orange robes, moved together, knee-bend for knee-bend, shoulder to shoulder, with rhythmic ease. Now I saw Holly's face clearly for the first time, and I thought for a second as my heart trembled that she saw me, too. The young man was handsome and in his early thirties, holding a stack of books between his right forearm and chest. They stepped forward and placed their order and in a moment, after they were served, started off down the busy street and disappeared in the crowd. She was gone. But the woman I thought I'd never see again had established some warbling new presence in my life. I strained my neck, peering through the press of bodies. It hardly mattered that she hadn't seen me or that I'd never lay eyes on her again and that it was unlikely that any thought of me crossed her mind more than once a year when conversation turned to failed love or the tumble of years. What mattered was that I'd been offered a glimpse into my younger heart.

As we moved across the green now, the strange sensation that I'd made contact with my past began to subside. The boys were hanging off my arms, half wrestling, taken in by the fair's high spirit. The leaves above our heads moved in a gentle rolling motion against the blue sky. I lifted Quinn over my shoulders and helicoptered him and let him down again and watched him wobble off in a dizzied circle.

We found our tent, a big white marquee, and gathered around were a hundred or more kids and parents. The man who'd been speaking with Holly Grey was standing beside the lectern talking to someone seated in the first row of stacking chairs. Finally the crowd began to settle, the people shuffling around and clearing their throats, and then Holly stood up from the front row and stepped to the microphone. She smiled, waiting for the audience to fall silent, and as she did I felt a strange and distant hope that we might both fall back in time, and those good years we'd shared would be ours again.

Holly was the editor of the books we'd come to have signed, and the author, she declared with familiar confidence, was a wonderful talent she took great pride in working with. She spoke briefly before introducing him, and twenty minutes later, after reading a few pages from his books, he invited everyone to the signing table where a line of young readers was already forming. By now the sun had moved behind the wall of buildings on the park's western edge. It was past four o'clock, and I was standing off to the side, thinking about that part of my life I'd shared with Holly and the slippage of time that beguiles us all, when I heard my name called.

"Charlie Bellerose? Oh my God. *Charlie*. I can't *believe* this!"

"Hey. Wow," I said. "What are you doing here?"

I had constructed conversations based on just such a chance meeting many times in my imagination. In these fantasies she was as I had always liked to remember her—warm, joyful, and welcoming. Of course I hadn't let her change one bit in these reveries. A lover from your past will retain all those youthful qualities that have long since fallen away from your own life. She will remain emergent and at the edge of all possibility, every bit as young as the day you met.

I had always wondered what I'd do and say in such a circumstance; and I wondered, too, if she still loved me, or at least the memory of me, as I still loved her, and if all those crises and banalities that occur over the course of your twenties and thirties would have shaped us similarly. Over the past twenty years I'd often felt the shuffle of memory and the small shift in the air that seemed to accompany this sensation and tried to remind myself that the nostalgia afflicting me wasn't so unusual—that a father and husband of my age might look back in wonder with good reason. And then the air would clear, and the nostalgia would vanish as quickly as it had come, these thoughts of my first love retreating again into the dim recesses of memory.

Now, on that September afternoon we embraced with what—a cautious enthusiasm? Certainly it was brief and self-conscious, as if we'd both agreed that a moment longer might have induced some unwelcome but familiar intimacy, that it was best to stay on the surface and in the moment.

"This is—oh my God," she said. "This is wonderful."

"It's great to see you. How are you?"

"Wow," she said, nodding and smiling. "This is really something."

These exclamations of disbelief and pleasure went on back and forth for a time, then I told her whom I was here with—I think I pointed to them in the queue—and said that the older of my nephews had read and loved everything by the author she'd just presented.

I led her over to my brother and his kids and introduced them, and we hovered there, the two of us almost blushing with possibility, I thought, and busied the air between us with talk about everything other than what really lay between us, which was, to my mind, nothing less grand or pressing than the eternal mystery of first love. Nate helped, thank goodness. He was at ease and polite and charming, as he always was with attractive women, and smiled and nodded when Holly told him we'd lived together for a time in Montreal and West Berlin back in the eighties. He said he remembered her, though I don't recall ever mentioning Holly to him, and I knew they'd never met.

Titus got his books signed—an act that seemed less impressive and exciting for him than I'd hoped—and afterward the five of us cut across the park, books in hand, Nate and the boys out front, Holly and I trailing behind. Once the initial surprise of our meeting was over, she seemed confident and relaxed and walked with a floating stride that made my own shuffling gait feel willfully flatfooted. She told me about the large publishing house she'd been working at for the past ten years and how she traveled more than she liked to but that she'd been in love with the book trade ever since the very first day of the internship she got soon after returning from Europe once our relationship ended.

"And you?" she said. "Language academies? That sounds fantastic. *Five* of them?"

"Four and a half, I'd say."

I'd already told her what had brought me back to the city after so long and how work on the new academy was coming along. Then I handed her a photograph of my daughter from my wallet.

"She's beautiful! Absolutely gorgeous. Where is she hiding? Is she here today?"

I went on to tell her that Ava lived with her mother in Madrid, which itself was a long story.

"That must be hard," she said, handing back the photograph. "Being so far away from your daughter."

"It's harder than I thought it would be." I was surprised by my truthfulness.

It was clear after only a few minutes there was something about Holly that Titus was drawn to, and I wondered if she could read me as easily as I could read my nephew. He was hovering, listening in. I'd noticed him turning his head, trying to catch what we were talking about. Maybe he was simply intrigued that his uncle had bumped into an old friend and that she seemed to possess some powerful allure. It might also have had something to do with the fact that this old friend of mine was a good-looking woman. I can't be sure of this. But I saw his eyes follow her with a direct and unguarded note of sexual longing. I wondered if he sensed something between Holly and me similar to what he'd felt between his mother and her new boyfriend, the man who occupied the part of her life recently vacated by his father.

We walked along a row of white booths and tents lined with books and faces, and suddenly Holly pointed and waved and said, "There they are!"

I was surprised—I don't know why—to hear she had a family. It seems absurd to recall that I hadn't asked her about this, and she hadn't volunteered as much, but I can appreciate now that some remote, shared part of us might have wanted to delay this revelation, if only for a few minutes more. But then her son, a tall, skinny, good-looking adolescent named Luke, came striding up, wearing a longboard strapped to the backpack he carried on his shoulders. "Hey guys, I found her," he called, and the face of a very pretty girl appeared beside his.

"Finally," the girl said.

This was Riley. She shook Nate's hand, then mine, and turned to her mother. "Where *were* you?"

Riley looked so very much like Holly that I found myself staring at her. She had long brown hair and freckles and such a natural and effortless beauty that I consciously forced myself to take my eyes off her for fear that I might embarrass her, or myself. As we stood beside Holly's children, I saw how we each had aged; and pressed against the flesh of youth, it was clear to me the best years of their lives still awaited them and ours were perhaps moving off into the distance faster than we cared to admit. It was an astonishing thought at that moment—now, not at all—but I remember the surprise that came when I understood that an ex-girlfriend of mine could have children so grown, so independent, so lovely. That I had a daughter of my own who was only three years younger than Riley didn't seem to lessen the impact of this realization. Titus and Quinn were now talking to Luke about his longboard, and his sister, who was quicker to smile, lingered at the edge of our grown-up conversation. I didn't know at the time that Riley and Luke were twins, fifteen years old. Luke was taller than his sister but looked at least a year older.

"Do you know where your dad is?" Holly asked her daughter, and then, as if on cue, a man emerged from the crowd carrying two bags of books.

"Look who I found, Glenn," Holly said. "Charlie Bellerose. You remember me telling you about Charlie. And this is Nate, Charlie's brother."

The man draped his left arm around his daughter's shoulder after setting the bags down on the grass. He was handsome, my height, with dark intelligent eyes, a minor dimple in the middle of his chin and long sideburns that marked him, I supposed, as a hip and current husband and father. The three boys were already four or five booths down from where we stood, talking to an artist—a young guy in an army jacket—seated behind a table and surrounded by drawings of colorful superheroes and villains. When we caught up with them, I saw the half-finished illustration the guy was laboring over, a wild screaming mouth at the centre of which snaked a forked tongue. He didn't raise or still his pencil as he cut his eyes up to the boys and answered their questions. On the wire display racks behind him were dozens of pictures of varying sizes, most of them fearsome-looking evildoers. Each frame was busy with action.

"There's no wall space left in Luke's bedroom," Holly said when I asked if I could buy one for him. "He's already got all those pretty girl singers up there. But thank you."

We embraced again, quickly, not much more than a close pat on the back, as her husband watched. I was aware that he wouldn't be sure what to make of me. Suspicion, of course, would've registered somewhere in the back of his mind. After he and my brother shook hands, and Nate removed himself from the small circle, I clasped his hand with the grip of an earnest and well-meaning businessman. I knew I would've felt uncomfortable if I'd been in his position. I didn't let my eyes leave his. "You have a beautiful family," I said. "You're a lucky man." I didn't think I'd see any of them ever again.

Two

A lot disappears from your memory in two decades. Things slip and fade and finally vanish. Places you've seen, people you knew, those wild revelations you thought would change your life. Where do they go? But there are things about my student days that I still remember perfectly—a view from a window, how an old friend moved when he was in a hurry, the autumn sunshine catching the bright white pages of a book turned open on a desk. Seeing Holly again brought that world back into sharp focus for me. It was like no time at all had passed since that weekend in Montreal when I first met her.

I'd gone to visit my best friend from high school, a boy by the name of Miles Esler. He was a brilliant kid, skinny with dark trusting eyes and a thick head of curly brown hair. He'd graduated a year ahead of our class and had an opinion concerning just about everything. It seemed to me that he got it right—whatever it was that took his imagination on any given day— most of the time. He could talk about the Beatles and make it sound like he'd sat in on the *Let It Be* sessions or explain how gasoline actually made your car run. School was too easy for him. He handed in brilliant assignments, got perfect grades in calculus and caused his teachers (I can only imagine) to think they had a prodigy on their hands.

At the end of the school day we'd take the streetcar down to Lake Ontario and smoke a joint sitting on the broken-up sidewalk cement and talk about getting the hell out of Toronto, which was as cold as it was boring in winter and as stifling as it was humid in summer. He wore a small diamond in his left ear, a fake, of course. The jocks left him alone because he wasn't a direct threat and because we pretty well kept to ourselves. I tried to come up with questions that would stump him. *What exactly is a hologram? How does lightning actually happen?* No one I knew could answer questions like those. But Miles, at the age of fifteen or sixteen, could explain the mathematics of these curiosities, scribbled formulas that meant nothing to me. He was offered a full-ride scholarship to study chemistry at a prestigious university in the United States but turned it down. Having grown up without a father, he said he wasn't going to abandon his mom like his old man had. The next province over was as far as he was willing to go. He'd be making serious money at some big research lab in five years anyway, he explained, with or without Stanford's help.

Miles and Holly met me at the bus station in Montreal. It was a cold, bright autumn afternoon, and a day of firsts. I'd never been to that city; nor, as I stepped off the bus, had I ever seen a woman as beautiful. I didn't know who she was or whom she was with or waiting for. It certainly didn't occur to me that she was with Miles, and the person she was waiting for was me.

He was waving his hand above the crowd when I saw him. Lugging my backpack, I pushed past a group of people, still wondering who the girl beside him was and thinking up some hungry boyish comment I could share with him the moment we were out of earshot. *Imagine waking up beside that every morning* or something along those lines. Little did I know. I smiled and glanced at her as Miles and I shook hands the way we thought old college buddies might do, with more eagerness and testosterone than we might normally have summoned—though surely warranted by the occasion—and then he slapped me on the back and said, "I want you to meet Holly." Looking as proud as I'd ever seen him, he put his arm around her waist and pulled her into him.

"Good to meet you," I said.

She leaned forward and kissed my cheek. I'd never been kissed on the cheek before. It was something they did in Paris.

"You look different from how I imagined you," she said, tucking a strand of chestnut-colored hair behind an ear. It had come loose from her ponytail. "Miles has been talking about you for*ever*."

He'd been gone only five weeks and already had a girlfriend who was talking about forever. This must have been some sort of campus record. Or did that happen here all the time? Maybe it was par for the course at a university like McGill. All the schools I was looking into at the time had their own particular reputation. Some were preppy, others were party schools; there were the heavily academic ones, and those devoted to granola and Birkenstocks. You heard about a few for the sheer number of beautiful girls who strolled between the buildings wearing tight jeans and adorable smiles. I'd heard there were a lot of pretty girls in Montreal. But this was off the charts.

Her pale complexion made the freckles on her face stand out, and the dark brown of her eyes—large and full of life—was flecked with gold.

"Nothing bad, I hope."

"Wouldn't you like to know!" she said, smiling.

I noticed the collection of pins on her lapel. "I guess we like the same bands," I said.

The left breast of her army surplus overcoat was clustered with music pins and two small flags, one British, the other German. It was a sort of postpunk tribute by the look of it. The Waterboys, Kraftwerk, the Smiths—the sort of mideighties stuff we were all listening to in those days. She didn't quite look the part, aside from the army surplus jacket. Tying her hair back in that ponytail seemed more preppy and clean-cut than anything. But I liked her taste in music because, well, it reflected my own.

What did I feel that day when I learned of their living arrangements? Envy, if not outright jealousy, I suppose. My best friend, a *peer*, was already living with a beautiful woman and enjoying what I could only imagine was the sort of boundless sex that surely went along with the rest of it. Technically Holly shared a room on campus with a Bermudan girl named Georgia and still made an appearance there once, maybe twice, a week. But this hardly dampened the wonder

I felt for my friend's situation. That his girlfriend was willing and able to sleep in his bed five nights out of seven impressed me terribly. I just couldn't believe it. He was the luckiest eighteen-year-old kid in the world. We'd talked endlessly about such things, of course— girls and women—but that he'd come as far as this in so little time was nothing short of miraculous. It was something to beat your chest and crow about. Miles, however, did no such thing. He hadn't even mentioned her on the two or three occasions we'd spoken on the phone while setting up that visit. For that reason he seemed all the more mature. It was as if the position he occupied now, that of the freshman with the beautiful girl on his arm, was a place he'd occupied all along and I'd just failed to notice.

After the introductions we walked through downtown on our way to my friend's apartment. The sidewalks and outdoor cafés were busy with people. The sky was clear and bright, and the October air pleasant. Shadows moved on the shops' plate-glass windows. Pretty girls were everywhere. I felt the excitement of the approaching weekend, the longing for sex, the promise that something in my life was going to change. I wondered if Miles and this new girl were already in love or if by some stroke of luck he'd stumbled upon a girl who sought out sex for its own sake, just because she liked it. I couldn't get over his good fortune. If fate could shift so swiftly for him, then it surely might offer me some similar opportunity that weekend. It was as if he had always known that something was waiting for him on the other side of the life we'd led back home, as if all the dreaming we'd done was little more than a preamble to the bigger and more interesting game that awaited. And it seemed he was right. In the splendor of Holly's feminine presence, and the fact that they were together now, I saw that he'd been right all along.

I tried not to stare that first day in Montreal. But I couldn't stop my eyes from wandering back to her again and again. She smiled easily, and the light scattering of freckles on the bridge of her nose and high cheekbones made her look as wholesome and cheerful as a summer's day. Her ponytail bobbed delicately as she walked, the way I imagined a ballerina's would.

In the heart of one of the student ghettos, the building they lived in was a three-story flat-roof town house of dull, tobacco-colored brick. On weekends, he said, it was usually just one big party up and down the street.

"Sounds like fun," I said.

"Oh yeah. You'll see."

I noticed bicycles chained up everywhere outside and in the entrance by the tenant mailboxes. The flat itself was small and dumpy and smelled vaguely of other people's food. The afternoon light falling through the windows turned its walls and the bamboo curtain separating the kitchen and living room a beautiful rich orange. The only object of any size familiar to me from Miles's house back home was his desk. It sat to the left of the door that led out to the small balcony looking over Rue de Bullion. I recognized it from his bedroom and knew its bottom left drawer as the place he'd stored his copies of *Hustler* and *Penthouse*. He didn't need to rely on those magazines anymore, though I still did. That was my first thought when I saw the desk, that he was miles ahead of me when it came to knowing anything about women.

"Welcome to the garret," he said.

I had already noticed the poem he was referring to, ten or fifteen lines called "The Garret" by Ezra Pound, scribbled out on a slip of brown paper taped to the wall beside a Pink Floyd poster. I imagined the hand-writing was Holly's.

We started drinking early that afternoon. We smoked a joint Miles had pulled from a jar he kept in the freezer and listened to some of the records he kept in milk cartons stacked in a corner. We listened to the Buzzcocks and New Order and The Jam and later made a big pot of spaghetti and ate it sitting on the pullout couch that had been designated mine for the weekend. I told them I didn't have any fake ID when Miles mentioned going out to the bars. He was turning a ball of pasta on his fork. "Not to worry. This, my friend, is Montreal."

We ventured from one end of downtown to the other, the city lights shining down over our faces and leather jackets as we passed old-time taverns and flashy new clubs along Saint-Laurent. In my memory I see a kid I barely recognize now—a tall, skinny boy at the beginning edge of his life, obviously underage, full of nervous expectation. The doormen and bouncers that night didn't care at all that I looked so young, just waved us through as if we'd been there a hundred times before. Each doorway was a portal leading into a world of beautiful girls. Of course I didn't know the names of any of the streets or bars or clubs we visited that night, but these would soon become familiar to me after I moved to Montreal the following year. Nor do I remember much about the band we saw at a club that night. I'd heard them on the radio once or twice playing a catchy song about life in the suburbs. What I do remember clearly is watching Miles kissing his new girlfriend as they danced next to the small stage and feeling happy that my best friend had everything you could ever want.

We finished the leftover spaghetti and tried to keep the fun going when we got home; but we couldn't drink anything more, and five minutes later I was passed out on the pullout couch. I don't know if I'd been asleep a few minutes or a few hours, but I woke up when I heard footsteps cross the apartment floor. I was disoriented. My head was pounding, and my ears were ringing after a night of loud bars and music. For a moment I didn't know where I was, and then when everything came clear again—that I was lying on Miles's couch in Montreal—I felt that something was going to happen. What I was hoping for surprised me. I hoped it was Holly standing there on the other side of that flimsy bamboo curtain and that she wouldn't go back into the bedroom she shared with my best friend. I wanted her to silently slip in beside me on the couch. I imagined her warm legs against mine and the taste of her lips and the feel of her hand reaching for my cock. I held my eyes closed and wished with all my heart that it was her and that she knew something about me before I knew it myself.

"You asleep?" Miles said.

"Yes."

He sat down on the floor, his back up against the pullout. "Come on. Wake up."

I ignored him.

"I'm too wired to sleep. My head's on fire. . . ."

After he didn't say anything for a few minutes, I began to think he'd fallen asleep propped up right there against the couch. I saw a faint light shining in the window when I opened my eyes.

He turned and looked at me over his shoulder. "You were walking with a cute girl last week. I talked to Anne a few days ago. She told me she saw you."

I used to call on Miles every morning on my way to school before he went off to Montreal. His mother— whom he sometimes called by her first name, Anne— usually answered the door holding a blue coffee mug and a cigarette. She was a secretary at some sort of electrical parts manufacturer. Miles didn't remember much about his father, only that he'd taken off when he was a baby. On Sunday mornings I used to see a different car in their driveway, and sometimes a man—rarely the same man twice—hovering about, watching the street from the front window as if he were expecting someone to drive into his life and complicate matters.

"A cute girl?" I said.

"That's right. Cute."

"That would have been Sandra."

"Vizinczey? The volleyball player?"

"Yeah," I said, still half asleep.

"That girl has some serious legs."

We spoke about Sandra for a little while longer, about her beautiful legs, and about some other people at school, girls and boys, and after Miles finally staggered back off to bed—I don't know how much later—I did my best to think about Sandra's legs. But all I could think about was Holly sleeping beside my best friend in the next room and what it must feel like to wake up beside a woman as perfect as she'd seemed to me that first day.

In the morning I found the note Miles had left on the kitchen table telling us when and where to meet him later that afternoon. There was a group project he was working on with some people from his biology class. He'd mentioned it the night before, but I'd forgotten this till now.

Holly and I went to their favorite diner for breakfast. We sat in a green booth at the back beside an old-time jukebox that no one put money in anymore. There were two ceiling fans that remained lifeless while we were there and a long desolate countertop where three old men sat and slowly turned their heads as the waitress came and went.

"It's our place," Holly said, opening the menu. "Greasy eggs galore." She was wearing a red bracelet on her left wrist and big blue earrings. Her eyes were shining and bright. She looked incredibly fresh and happy. "Best hangover eggs in town," she said.

"I'll be trying those, then. I guess you know all the best places in Montreal by now."

"I like it better than where I grew up, anyway," she said. I asked her where that was. It was a town back in Ontario I'd never heard of.

"I guess Montreal's better than most places you can come from," I said.

The waitress appeared again, this time with coffee, and asked if we were ready to order. Once she left, Holly said, "You know what? Your French isn't all that bad. Better than mine when I got here. Anyway, I'm not staying in Montreal forever." She put a teaspoon of sugar in her coffee and stirred it, then looked out the window for a few seconds before turning back to me. "There's too much to see everywhere else in the world," she said. "I really believe that. People like to stay where they are. That's what I don't get. All those people out there . . ." She paused again and watched the crowd passing by on the sidewalk. "They wake up in their beds and convince themselves that wherever they are is the only place in the world. I don't get that."

"That's just natural, right?" I said. "Wanting to be comfortable?"

"Maybe when you're old, sure. I get that. When you're old you want to stop and think about all the things you've done in your life. That's fine. But when you're young? Do you want to hear what my worst fear in life is?"

"Shoot."

"Getting old and being full of regret. Hating myself for not taking chances. I want to be able to look back on my life and not wish things had been different. You only go around once, right?"

The waitress loaded the table between us with plates and glasses of orange juice and refilled our mugs with coffee. By now it was probably noon, and I was starving and still slightly hungover, though not so badly that I wasn't able to appreciate the comments Holly had made. She went on to explain that she thought people ended up living cruel or unsatisfying lives because they confined themselves to the present. It was a question of taking a longer view and regarding your world through the prism of your older self.

"Do you think you could actually do that?" I said. "It takes a lot of concentration to walk around all day wondering about consequences and what you're going to be thinking forty years from now. It might take all the fun out of things, too."

"I didn't say it would be easy. I guess that's the point, right? I'd call that an essential moral dictate. You've got to figure out how to live a good life."

"Okay, whatever that means." I had never heard anyone talk about essential moral dictates before.

"I'm reading a lot of Kant these days," she said. "It's sort of like his categorical imperative. Which hinges on the belief that the idea is inside all of us. You've got to recognize it and bring it to the surface and actually do something about it."

She went on to tell me about her German classes.

She'd just finished reading *The Threepenny Opera* and *All Quiet on the Western Front* for a course called Twentieth-Century German Literature. The only German novel I'd ever read in my life was by some stroke of good fortune the Remarque novel. We talked about it a little, but mostly I listened. Her confidence and intelligence about books were something I'd never witnessed before. Excited and smart, she picked apart that Remarque novel in a way that made me want to read it all over again. When she mentioned Bertolt Brecht, I told her the only play I really knew anything about was *The Pajama Game.*

She made a funny face. "Why's that?" she said, picking up a piece of buttered toast.

"There was a girl I liked. She was an actress and she had a part in it."

"Miles never told me you were an actor. But I can see that. You have expressive eyes."

"I've never acted in anything myself. The idea of standing in front of a whole bunch of people like that terrifies me. That's absolutely the worst thing I can imagine. I have nightmares about being up in front of people and forgetting my lines. I don't know how they do that. Actors, I mean."

"You never know until you try."

"Maybe. But I used to watch all these rehearsals she was involved in. Every day after school I'd find some excuse to hang around the auditorium, where they were rehearsing. It was just a typical school play, and probably horrible. But I thought she was amazing. I have no idea where she is now. She went off to some performing arts school last year."

"You're a romantic, I think," she said. "I like that." She was mopping up the egg yolk on her plate with the last of her toast.

"Maybe I am. It's hard to say. But I could never talk to her. She had guys falling all over her all the time. I'm not so great with girls."

She popped the toast into her mouth, chewed and swallowed, then sipped her coffee. I'd never seen a girl eat so much.

"That's not so strange," she said. "You build someone up so much and end up being tongue-tied the whole time. I know what that's like."

She was too beautiful and confident to ever be tongue-tied in front of anyone, I thought as she dabbed at the corners of her mouth with a serviette. So smart and at ease with herself, she wasn't nearly self-conscious enough to worry about what people thought of her.

"And then they become unapproachable, right?" I said. "For me, anyway. I think I was probably in love with the *idea* of her more than the actual person. She was hot, though."

Holly smiled and slipped the serviette under her right thigh and reached two fingers into her shirt pocket.

"Looks like you were hungry," I said.

"I'm definitely a breakfast person."

She took a stick of lip balm out of her pocket and applied it, then slipped it back into her pocket.

I looked at my watch. It was almost one o'clock. "I think I could get used to university life."

"We have a bit of time to have some fun," she said. "It's not all categorical imperatives."

"It better not be," I said.

We paid the waitress and walked over to the campus to meet Miles. He was standing in front of the Social Sciences Building with a squash racquet sticking out of his backpack. She kissed his face, and then he shook my hand.

"Welcome to the first day of the rest of your life," he said.

⇥ Three

The renovations at the academy
were going full-bore by the time Holly stepped back
into my life. I was already in over my head, but for
a few days after that chance encounter I couldn't get
my mind back into the here and now. Everywhere I
went, and at all hours, I felt her presence as strongly as
if she'd left the room only a moment before. My car-
penters hammered and banged away as I tried to drag
myself back into my work. I ground through bank
statements and city red tape, conferenced with the
other academies and started firming up contracts for
the winter term. At lunch break I joined the carpen-
ters, submarine sandwich in hand, and talked about La
Liga and David Beckham's declining fortunes at Real
Madrid. But I couldn't keep my mind on soccer. I was
thinking about Holly Grey.

After locking up for the day, I'd head for home, a
fifteen-minute bike ride, and I always half expected
to see her—at every street corner, behind the windshield of each passing car. I kept my eyes peeled like a
man waiting for a secret message to be delivered. I rode
along Gerrard and through Cabbagetown watching for
her. I barreled down the grassy hill by the Riverdale
petting farm into the Don Valley, where urban legend

had it that deer were still spotted occasionally and forty years ago the roar of the lion housed at the now-closed zoo had echoed through the shallow depths. I looked for her there among picnicking couples and solitary women walking dogs or jogging along pathways. Back up on the other side I'd stop in Little Chinatown to buy some meat or fish and vegetables, looking for her there, too, when picking through a bin of oranges or standing by a lobster tank. And finally I'd cycle the last stretch home through the park where the boys and Nate and I sometimes played soccer and tossed the Frisbee, and never once did I see her. But I knew I would. It was only a matter of time.

Everywhere around me marriages were shattering like old china dolls, and still the world rolled merrily along. What did it matter? Back in Madrid, well-meaning friends had assured me that my daughter would be fine in the end. Kids were more resilient than we thought. With a few adjustments it could be a good year, they said, maybe even a beautiful year. That's what I'd tried to convince myself of before coming over. I saw myself flying back into Madrid every month or so to book a suite at the Reina Victoria. I'd always be Ava's father, nothing would change that, and she was old enough to figure out the truth of the situation, which was that her parents could love her separately as much as they did together, maybe even more so.

On paper it all looked eminently doable. What I had to do was stick to the plan. It was a wonderfully real and achievable prospect and no less a desire than it was my right. I'd imagined myself straddling two worlds— a controlled and confident tightrope walker crossing back and forth over the Atlantic bearing presents and renewed energy, the transformation from hungry bachelor to family man completed seamlessly somewhere between takeoff and landing. It was as good as a done deal. A new life beckoned me. It would be like falling into the arms of a beautiful woman.

I was determined to keep up my guard, stay healthy and focus on the job that had brought me here. I'd get that fifth academy up and running, and in the meantime I'd hit the gym four days out of seven, cook myself sensible meals and limit myself to a reasonable amount of alcohol at night. I reminded myself constantly that I'd return to Madrid in a year's time, not a day longer. It was a question of getting through it, focusing the mind and knowing this was not the end of anything. I even started reading novels again, after not reading for a decade. This was all part of the routine I needed to keep myself going, ten pages a night whether I liked it or not. I bought myself a mountain bike, took out a membership at the downtown YMCA and picked up a big fat recipe book especially tailored to the health-conscious professional. By half past five every morning I was out the door and heading to the Don Valley for an hour-long trail ride. Into the fall season the valley trails were busy with joggers and fellow cyclists who emerged like phantoms from banks of fog on those early mornings, and I'd often find a tired pod of salmon pooling below an obstacle in the river, rallying their forces before forging on. I would stop and observe this marvelous scene. And if one did jump and made it instead of being pushed back to try again later, I considered myself and the day privileged, as if I'd just caught a falling star. Its dorsal fin would disappear into the water with exhausted triumph on the other side of those rocks, and I'd watch and wait for the next one and cast around in my mind for some image or memory of Ava that would carry me through to the end of my day. What didn't go unnoticed was the instructive symbolism of the spectacle before me, those desperate twisting efforts to get home.

In the late afternoon I'd hover over my Skype page waiting for signs of my daughter. I sent barrages of e-mails with attached photos of past family vacations, birthday parties and hiking trips, moments whose significance grew for me with each passing week. I found myself looking at these obsessively. If it wasn't later than five o'clock, her image would materialize before me like some electronic angel, imperfectly grainy and smiling and full of infinite mercy. "There you are!" I'd say, and when I detected no note of melancholy or despair or resentment in her voice or eyes I was able to forget for a few moments that we were separated by a black and churning ocean as fathomless as the decision I'd made to leave her behind.

One afternoon I told her some stupid lie about everything being the same as it had always been. "Yeah. I guess you're right," she said. "I guess that's why I'm talking into a computer right now." And then she slammed the connection shut in my face. When I tried to raise her again, she didn't answer. She didn't answer her cell phone, either. I put my head in my hands and waited. After half an hour I went out to the living room and poured myself a drink. It was three days before she answered another Skype request.

It didn't take long for the reality of single life to set in. Time away from Ava felt like a cruel and selfish retreat from the one pure thing in my life. I could only fool myself for so long. I needed to get back, but I didn't know how. The fantasies that had sustained me guttered. I confided this to my brother, who actually listened without expressing the need to start cursing his own circumstances. He asked if I thought things would be any better if I hadn't left. What's different? he said.

I didn't tell Nate about my growing obsession with Holly or the past we shared. Instead we sat up talking about the plans I'd devised to break into the city's competitive language market. He had a good business head on his shoulders and gave me his take on things. There were three schools within a ten-minute walk of the new academy. Two of them were not-for-profit organizations, catering to a completely different clientele and mortally dependent on the caprices of provincial and federal funding. The third had a heavy emphasis on Latin America. I'd visited each one, shaken hands with the directors, had a look around. The main competition as far as I was concerned was a fourth school up on Bloor Street, beyond my blast radius. They had their hooks into all the same markets we did, and some we didn't—principally, a newly implemented ten-year bursary cash cow out of Riyadh that had just started sending Saudi kids to Toronto by the planeload.

"Sounds like that's some low-hanging fruit," Nate said.

He was right, but pursuing a contract as rich as that was also the sort of commitment that demanded more time and focus than I had on hand. In a year or two that's exactly the kind of expansion I was aiming for. But right now I was overloaded. Apart from managing the renovations, I'd started assembling the team for the new academy—sales and marketing managers, accounts administrators, accommodation and social activities organizers, program director—looking exclusively for people from within the industry who knew the business and could run a department with limited or no oversight the minute they walked through the front door.

After that week I stayed with Nate, we didn't talk so much about the past. It was always there between us, of course. But it would serve neither of us to go too deeply into it or to dwell on it. As I said, we'd been taken in by an uncle after our parents died. Hugo was a quiet man, a city engineer and our father's only brother. I recall few details from this time. It might simply be characterized as a lost year in my life. I was going into ninth grade when this happened, and I can only imagine myself as I might have appeared then, a new kid in a new school, standing forlornly in the throng of boys and girls rife and dripping with the high spirits of youth. If nothing had made sense to me when I still had parents to turn to (and likely nothing did) neither had the world asked anything of me yet. After they died its demands were ceaseless and unendurable. Nothing made any sense to me at all. Our uncle was a kind man but unequipped for the challenge. Who might have been suitably equipped, I have no idea. But I was a special case, it seemed. Nate handled the situation with an astonishing calm. He made friends within weeks after we were transferred into our new school district. I couldn't understand this. I do remember some specifics—his smile, for example, as he leaned against his locker door between classes. It looked like he didn't have a care in the world. I'd stare at him until he noticed me, then he'd give me a smile so fraudulent that I almost thought he was a complete stranger. We shared a bedroom on the third floor of my uncle's house, a tall narrow semi on a quiet avenue just north of Bloor Street. Every night for months I tried to talk about our parents. I needed to know that I wasn't alone, to hear that my brother and I shared something no one else could understand. But the deeper I tried to drill down, the more he told me that this was our life now and talking about them all night wasn't going to bring them back.

Nor did we talk about that last night in Madrid when he'd taken that wild swing at me. This old news had been softened by the passage of time. We'd both decided that too many important things had happened since then. We had adult concerns now and were pleased to concentrate on the moment and, better yet, the future—to show each other the best of what we had to offer, to illustrate the undiminished quality of our dreams and aspirations. Our father and mother came up, of course, but in the unreal and dimly remembered terms that come to grown children who lose their parents far too early. It was "Remember when Dad used to . . ." and "Mom always liked it when . . ."

At night I lay awake wondering if Holly wasn't waiting for a sign from me. That meeting seemed too perfect and meaningful to be anything less than predestined. I was reaching, obviously. I appreciate that now. But here I was, newly single and casting about in the city of my youth, and out from the past steps my first love. On one level I knew how unrealistic it all was; yet the fantasy of stepping back in time with her played on in my head. I found myself thinking about this at all hours of the day and night. Hovering over my keyboard after a long day, I learned the name and location of the office building where she worked and the long list of books she'd published in her career. There were photographs of Holly smiling for the camera at glitzy parties, galas and prize-giving ceremonies. One afternoon I caught myself picking up the phone about to call her office before I stopped myself. So instead of stepping back into the safety of the past, I stepped out onto the streets and began to call in on half a dozen shops or restaurants every day to present my business card and talk about how I'd be bringing some new foot traffic into the neighborhood—the sort of common-sense meet-and-greet, low-intensity PR campaign I'd used for each of my previous start-ups.

One windy afternoon a heavyset Sikh sporting a magnificent grey beard examined my card with unusual interest after we shook hands. His name was Paul, and he owned and operated the electronics shop two blocks north of me, presiding over a thousand square feet of oversize flat screens that played endless loops of high-definition golf greens, hang-gliding adventures and the dancing turbulence of the Great Barrier Reef. "Oh, you are most welcome to the neighborhood, sir," he said with a smile, slipping the card into his breast pocket. "My brother is also involved in the language business. He is a translator in New Delhi. The greatest of cities. He is accredited in nine languages. Perhaps you will be interested in joining the Downtown Business Council?"

After Paul loaded me up with the relevant documents, I dipped into the Starbucks three floors below the academy and saw the woman who at this time of day often sat reading at the table beneath the big Picasso print on the exposed brick of the west wall. She was an attractive thirty-something, I guessed, and sometimes she looked up from her book and smiled when she saw me. I thought maybe she'd help push the thoughts of Holly out of my head. She was there almost every afternoon, sitting alone, a silver bracelet flashing against her tan skin as she sipped her chai latte. I was feeling connected, possibly even gregarious, my new association with Paul at the electronics shop having buoyed me with a high sense of community spirit.

"Nice little niche you've found yourself," I said.

She lifted her eyes to mine. They were quite beautiful, I thought, and showed surprise, then impatience and last, a small measure of sympathy.

"Sorry. I've got to do this," she said, indicating the paperwork spread out before her.

"You bet," I said. "I know the feeling."

I joined the queue, chastened, and even before my coffee was served, she collected her things and walked out the door.

⇥ Four

Nate came to Montreal
for a lacrosse tournament in the fall of my second year
at McGill. At the time I was living with three engineering students in an old house on Rue Jeanne-Mance, a
place that reeked of moldy insulation and damp plaster once the furnace was turned on in the fall, and
somehow that smell lingered on through the winter
until spring came and the windows were opened to
let in the freshness of a new season. The dining room
table, a slab of unfinished particle board, sagged per-
ceptibly, like the belly of a fat old fish. My roommates,
all of whom were two years ahead of me, had known
one another since their first weeks at McGill. They
spent their days at lectures and studying at the library.
As a result I hardly saw them, and they paid very little
attention to me when I did. On occasion Stevens, who
lifted weights in his bedroom, which was right beside
mine, leaned a sweaty shoulder against my door frame
and told me that I was welcome to tag along to one
of their engineering parties. "Looks like you could
use a piece of tail, Bellerose," he'd say, and I'd tell him
thanks, but I was all right for now. On Saturday mornings they played ball hockey in the house league and
afterward went off drinking for the rest of the day. I

cleared out on the weekends they brought the team back to the house. I'd go to the pool on campus or find a carrel at the library and read all day. There was always a stack of novels I had to get through. During the week they studied incessantly and rarely got home before midnight. I admired how they could turn that switch on and off in their heads.

It was a Thursday night when my brother called. I was home alone—doing what, I can't remember—but I know I was alone. I'd just broken it off with Sandra, the volleyball player. We had decided to go to the same university after a couple of good months together in high school, and things hadn't worked out as well as we'd hoped. When I answered the phone, I heard my brother's voice. Two years had passed since we'd last seen each other. "Uncle Hugh gave me your number. He figured I should give you a call. So I'm calling."

His team, the Syracuse Orange, had been eliminated in the second round of the conference finals, and now he was sitting in a dumpy hotel room somewhere downtown with a couple of his teammates watching TV and drinking Courvoisier. I heard noises in the background, loud talking and laughing, and a girl's voice. Nate had captained the lacrosse team in high school and won most of the medals and ribbons that counted, and now he was trying to do the same in university. I couldn't remember a time when he wasn't surrounded by girls. He knew how to talk to them, and what to say, and after some exchange in the school hallway—chuckling to himself as he sauntered past my locker, where I stood helpless, two years his junior and in awe—he would turn to the girl I was trying to talk to, or to the girl two lockers down who smiled at me from time to time, and whom I dreamed of at night, and he'd talk to her effortlessly or make a wisecrack at my expense that made her laugh and look at her feet and forget all about me once he walked off down the hall. It was like a game to him. When he ended up winning a lacrosse scholarship to Syracuse University, I was relieved to see him go.

Nate's hotel was in a part of the city I wasn't familiar with. It was a cold night, and the taxi's headlights caught the colors of the leaves drifting over the street, and when the driver finally found the address Nate had provided, I saw the billboard he'd told me to look for. Situated over an abandoned parking lot and fastened to the side of the hotel, it showed a pretty model's face, an advertisement for an optometrist, I think.

I wished I was at home reading or at Miles and Holly's apartment. I was over there once or twice a week in those days. But I felt I should make the effort to see my brother. In fact, I almost tricked myself into believing that he'd come all the way from Syracuse to visit me, though obviously it was a lacrosse tournament that had brought him here.

When I got to his room on the fifth floor, he introduced me to the girl whose voice I'd heard over the phone. Her back up against the headboard, she was sitting on the bed, legs crossed at the ankles. She had a very attractive face. "My name's Bunny," she told me.

Nate beamed ecstatically. "Bunny! Can you believe that? We have Bunny here with us this evening."

Going Home Again

She worked at the strip club where they'd spent the afternoon. Her hair touched the tops of her shoulders, and her bangs were cut high and straight across her forehead. Her fingernails were painted in an alternating black-and-white pattern, almost akin to a piano keyboard, and when Nate introduced me she smiled and said, "Hello, little brother."

The other two people in the room that night were, like him, forwards—attackmen, in lacrosse parlance—and they all played together on the same line. One of them explained how they roamed around the opponent's half of the field waiting to pounce, always pressing. They were predators, he said. It was instinct, nothing thought out, nothing verbal. You exploited the moment. At any instant each knew where the other two were on the field. That night it looked like they had that same nonverbal communication going on. The hotel room was like a playing field, and Bunny was the object of their attack. Without needing to speak or make eye contact, they chucked beers to one another and traded high fives, and when Pete—the dark-haired one who'd explained the magic of the game—took Bunny into the washroom and locked the door, my brother smiled and slid down against the headboard and folded his hands over his chest with a look of great satisfaction on his face, like he himself had just scored the winning goal.

She went around to each of us that night, and when it was my turn, Bunny grabbed her small leather purse and led me into the bathroom and closed the door behind us. I got out my money and gave it to her. She counted it and put it in her purse, then sat on the edge of the tub and opened my fly. I watched the top of her head for as long as I could, then closed my eyes. She didn't want to embarrass me. Everything happened very fast. When she was through, she slipped the red purse off her shoulder again and took out a paperback copy of *L'Étranger* and started reading. I did myself back up and leaned against the tiled wall and watched her. She might have been waiting for a bus or for a waiter to bring her a burger and plate of fries. I hadn't needed as much time as my brother or his friends had, though we waited like that for as long as the others had taken. Her checkered black-and-white fingernails looked beautiful and modern against the dull, scuffed cover of her book. She mouthed the words as they came to her and rolled each page softly between her fingertips before turning it.

Later that night I lay in bed and thought about doing all the things I hadn't done with Bunny and wanted to do now. I'd wanted to hold my eyes open and look into her eyes when I came, to strip off her clothes and explore her body. But none of that had happened. My mind raced that night. We'd finally gone back out into the main room after enough time had passed, and soon after that I took a cab home.

My brother had smiled, slapped me on the back and said, "Okay, stud. Go home and get some beauty rest."

I told Miles I was thinking about dropping out and going traveling. This was a few weeks after Nate's visit.

"Why would you do that?" he said.

"I don't know. I guess I'm just bored."

We were sitting at one of those old beer halls with great big round tables that seat twenty or twenty-five people. It was loud, everyone talking and laughing. I think midterms might have been winding down just then. Students were out celebrating, getting drunk and looking for sex. MTV videos were blaring on a big screen at one end of the room, and we were forced to raise our voices to hear each other.

"Okay," he said. "So what's stopping you?"

"That's the weird part. I can't think of anything."

"What's even weirder is if you stuck it out here just to get some stupid piece of paper with your name on it."

He was right.

I went to the Office of the Registrar after a few days of debating this and gave notice that I was dropping my courses. When they told me I'd be entitled to a refund for the spring term, I decided to put that money toward my plane ticket.

That night I told my roommate Stevens what I had in mind. He had a friend who'd just moved out of his girlfriend's apartment and needed a place, so my moving out wasn't a problem, and I was welcome to leave as soon as I wanted. The next day I cleared out my things, got my rent deposit back and moved in with Miles and Holly. Four days later I bought my ticket to Athens. It was a cold afternoon, the temperature having fallen by fifteen degrees in the space of twenty-four hours. I felt like I'd just won the lottery. "But somehow it doesn't feel real yet," I told Miles. "So far that ticket's just another piece of paper."

"It'll take you farther than a university degree," he said.

I walked over to the *dépanneur* two blocks away to pick up something for the three of us to eat and drink that evening. A pleasant mid-November snow was falling over the city, sparkling in the glare of the streetlamps and swirling in the headlights of passing cars. I bought two roast chickens, a bag of frozen French fries and some wine and beer, and as I walked back, bottles clinking in the bag, I considered my good fortune. In a week's time I'd be sitting in a square in Athens or nosing around the Parthenon or ferrying out in the direction of one of those mythical islands. The only thing I didn't understand was why it had taken me so long to take that step.

We opened the wine and tucked into our meal, and once the wine was finished we switched to beer, and then Miles brought out the bottle of grappa he'd been saving for a special occasion. We were sitting at the small table they'd set up beside the bamboo curtain, and by now it was overflowing with glasses and plates and bottles. The Waterboys were playing on the turntable. At the time it was Miles and Holly's favorite record.

"I don't think I'll need to eat for a year," I said.

"That was some serious food," Miles said.

"You're going to need reinforcements in Greece," Holly said, smiling radiantly. "You're going to need some help over there."

I told them I was counting on it.

"Every day you'll look out a window and see the Mediterranean," Miles said, following the song's drumbeat by slapping his hands against his knees. "In my book that's as close as you can get to heaven without actually dying. It probably snows there once every hundred years."

"I'd sure like to see it," Holly said.

"You will," I said. "We'll all see it together. I'm leaving a bit sooner than you guys is all."

We'd talked about them coming over next year and the three of us renting a stone house on an island and living some sort of Leonard Cohen lifestyle. We had no dates, only the fantasy that we were reaching out into the world together and would find and hold something that would be ours forever and we'd be different than everyone else. It was what the song Miles was drumming on his knees was about, and what Holly had been getting at when she took me to their favorite diner my first weekend in Montreal two years earlier. Take some chances, she'd said, since you only go around once. She wasn't going to be the sort of person to look back on her life with regret, none of us was. Such was the promise of our youth.

A thin layer of ice had formed in the toilet bowl during the night. The next morning the thermostat read eight degrees Celsius. One of us had left the window open in the washroom. I'd soon be far away from this frigid cold, I thought, but I didn't have the energy to think for long about my coming adventure. I just had to get through the day. I had one of those crippling hangovers that drags you along in its wake, selfish and demoralizing in its all-consuming physical ache. I closed the washroom window, took two Tylenols and lay back down on the couch. I slept for another hour, then got up and tried to watch a bit of TV and eat a sliver of toast. At around two that afternoon I cycled over to the gym.

It was frigid outside—the snow had stopped falling—and I began to feel like myself again. I had access to the squash courts and swimming pool despite having dropped out, since I still had my student ID. That afternoon I swam twenty slow lengths and then, exhausted, sat in the sauna with my eyes closed and felt the alcohol pour out of my skin. People came and went. I tried to think about Greece again, and the beaches, and all the girls I was going to meet. The sauna was packed with guys sitting there silently looking down at their feet. I think all the school's partiers went in there to sober up on Sunday afternoons. The steam carried the nauseating smell of alcohol. I buried my head under my towel and wished the day away.

It was after five when I got back to the apartment and found Holly sitting on the floor, cradling a mug of tea in her hands. She had a worried look on her face.

"Miles was gone when I woke up. He's still not here."

"I wouldn't worry about it," I said. "He's probably crashed out at the library, sound asleep on a stack of chemistry textbooks."

Going Home Again

The apartment was quiet for a few hours. I was sitting on the couch underlining places and things I wanted to see in the *Let's Go Greece* I'd been carrying around for weeks. Holly sat at the far end of the couch dipping in and out of *The Magic Mountain*. It was obvious that she wasn't able to focus. By now I was also starting to think it was strange that Miles wasn't home yet and that he hadn't called to say where he was. Then around eight o'clock two police officers came to the door, two big Francophones with mustaches and worried expressions. They asked us if Miles Esler lived here. Yes, we told them, he did. When I asked what the problem was, they said he'd been found in the north end of the city. He had fallen thirty feet from a pedestrian footbridge. My best friend was dead.

→∦ Five

I thought constantly about my father and mother in the weeks that followed. All I had left of them by now were memories and a few keepsakes and photographs. They didn't add up to much. Not enough, anyway. I knew what to expect after Miles died: the same thing. Over time all those details that were still so fresh in my head would start slipping away. That terrified me. I tried to recall specific moments and burn them into my memory, things we'd done together, conversations we'd had. Him leaning up against the couch in his apartment and talking that first night I stayed over. I thought about those afternoons we'd spent after school down by the lakeshore watching the gulls and talking about music and girls and getting out of Toronto. I tried to burn his memory into my brain. I promised myself over and over that I'd never let myself forget him. I created lists in my head of things we'd done, places we'd been to, things we'd talked about. Each of these categories spun off in dozens of different directions, each of which I charted as meticulously as someone moving along various branching paths that carried him deeper and deeper into some mystery. I could not let these memories fade as I'd let certain memories of my parents slip away. I remembered them now as people I'd once known and loved deeply, but always flittering about was the odd sensation that I'd made them up out of thin air, that their lives had been as fleeting as a dream. I don't mean to say I doubted they had ever lived and loved me and helped make me who I was. But had they really known me? Had I known *them*? I was a boy when they died. And that boy was a stranger to me now. When I tried to remember them, I pictured the family together and where I would have stood, but seeing my old self, I recognized only the surface of this person. I could not imagine myself fully into that family portrait.

I recalled that my mother wore her hair as all mothers did at that time, cut short with high bangs, and that my father, a carpenter, seemed unable to sit still. He was always busy, always at work. He had come from Belgium at the age of twelve and met my mother in 1958 at the age of twenty-two at a Victoria Day fireworks display. At the public park where they later took their young sons for picnics and Easter-egg hunts, they watched rockets explode over Lake Ontario. This story had been told to me a number of times. My father, by then apprenticed at the shipyard, led his shy date away from the crowd gathered there, and together they stood in darkness at the edge of the water and watched mesmerized, hearts agallop, as if the invention of the world were at hand. This was a moment of first love, my mother assured me. In another memory I am feverish and lying under a blanket watching television. I was home from school. My father returned much earlier from work than he normally did and surprised me with a can of ginger ale, the first pop I ever tasted. Who remembers their first soft drink, that explosive sugary fizz? He sat on the edge of the couch and slipped the white straw he'd taken from his shirt pocket into the can and told me to take a sip. He smelled of wood shavings and still might've had sawdust caught in his eyebrows. He was the handsomest man I knew. On that afternoon he took his carpenter's pencil out from behind his ear and stuck it in the can with my straw and pretended to drink.

The cemetery grounds on the day of the funeral were covered in a light dusting of snow. There was no birdsong in the air, and the trees were bare and grey. Miles's uncles and aunts and his mother's friends all knew that his last night had been spent with me and Holly. I couldn't help thinking that each and every one of them held the two of us responsible for his death. Though no one said anything of the sort, I just couldn't shake the feeling. After we each let a small shovelful of soil fall into the grave, Holly and I walked to the gravel road we would follow back to the cars. Miles's mother approached us as we stood there waiting for our ride. Her face looked washed out and pale; she had dark circles under her eyes. We'd already spoken about the night Miles died. I didn't know then that she'd never have the answer as to whether her son had jumped or fallen, but at the time she needed to believe his death was an accident, as I myself did. I didn't lie when Mrs. Esler asked me what I knew. I told her what I could, that we'd been celebrating and had gotten very drunk and that he'd left the apartment after I fell asleep. She asked if he'd been depressed or had said anything that might indicate something was wrong. I told her that he'd been the Miles I had always known and loved.

Now at the edge of the cemetery she told me and Holly that we were the two people her son had loved most in the world and that it was our job to carry his memory with us forever. I promised her I would. Holly cried and put her hand over her mouth, and Mrs. Esler touched my face with the tips of her fingers, then turned and walked down the path, back in the direction of the grave.

We drove Miles's mother from Toronto to Montreal two days later. She sat in the passenger seat holding his high school graduation portrait the whole time. I was driving, but it was her car—the blue Impala he and I had driven around the city, listening to music and hoping to meet girls. Holly was staring out the side window from the backseat. I tried to make eye contact with her in the rearview, though she never once looked up. We drove for six straight hours without saying a word, and when we got into Montreal, we packed his clothes and books and papers into boxes. Still, to me it felt like he might walk through the door at any minute. His mother left his furniture and his records. "He would've wanted you to have them," she said.

One afternoon a week later I was approached by two strangers in the street. It took me a moment to understand that they weren't from here and that I had no clue either as to where I was. Only when they asked for directions to Schwartz's Deli did I snap out of the spell I'd been walking under. They wore the expectant and pleased look of people on vacation in a place they've never been before. After I got my bearings, I pointed them in the right direction, and that's when it occurred to me that I was supposed to be somewhere else. My plane had left for Greece without me, carrying with it my dream of a wider world.

These meandering walks quickly became a daily ritual. I'd leave the apartment before sunup and walk for eight or nine hours. Half the time I didn't have any destinations in mind. I usually found a café or restaurant to break up these long and exhausting days. But more often than not I found it best to keep walking; it was a much better distraction, with the mind focused outward on the next street ahead or the shops I passed or the people I saw. Sometimes I saw Miles waiting at an intersection or standing in the window of a *dépanneur*, then I'd look again and he was gone.

I discovered that the city hadn't changed after my friend's death and offered no outward sign of this great loss. No one seemed to care. The streetlights still burned pleasantly that winter. People with expectant smiles passed me in the street. The falling snow glittered in the storefront lights along the Rue Saint-Hubert. I had nowhere to go now. I barely saw Holly the rest of that winter, though I slept on her couch every night.

Then, a few days after watching the *Challenger* disaster on television, I knew something had to change. I went out and found a job teaching ESL with the continuing-education program of the Montreal District School Board. It was volunteer work, but that didn't matter. I needed to do something with myself. Seeing those astronauts die on live TV served to confuse me even more than I already was. I was alone in a universe of random chaos and didn't know which way to turn. If something didn't change soon, I knew the hopelessness I was sinking into deeper and deeper was going to end up becoming a permanent state of being.

Holly was usually gone when I got up in the morning, and when I got home in the evening, her bedroom door was shut tight. I had no idea if she was in there or not. On the rare occasion I saw her, on a Saturday or Sunday afternoon, we didn't speak. She couldn't even look at me. An invisible wall had been put up between us, for reasons I couldn't grasp or ask her about.

One rainy spring day I walked out to the footbridge and leaned over the handrail. It spanned a one-lane road that carried traffic to a thickly treed neighborhood farther along. A car approached and passed beneath me, then everything was silent again. The bridge seemed to emerge organically from the sides of the valley it spanned. The ironwork was painted green, and the rust spots, long red teardrops staining the horizontal girders, pointed down like arrows. Miles and I had crossed it many times together, and now I tried to recall if he'd said anything I should've taken some deeper meaning from.

One morning I lay on the pullout couch, head buried under a pillow, listening to Holly get ready for her day. She walked back and forth through the small apartment much as she had that first weekend I'd stayed there. I didn't think about her slipping into bed with me now. That was gone. I fantasized about her simply acknowledging me, taking notice, offering a simple gesture, a smile. I couldn't understand the anger she felt. It all seemed directed toward me, almost as if I'd pushed him to his death. I listened to her naked feet treading the floor and dreamed about going away and starting my life over far away from the cold that had settled between us. When the door closed behind her, I stood by the window looking down over the street and drew a face in the condensation on the window. The face had no mouth. I found a scrap of paper and drew a rough image of the footbridge Miles had fallen from. I scratched it out and turned the page and sketched another face. I put on some music, brewed a pot of coffee and filled the rest of the notebook. I started drawing every morning after Holly left for class. I only worked a few hours in the afternoon three days a week, so free time was one of my problems. I'd put on one of Miles's records, flip open one of those pads and disappear into my imagination. I didn't have the concentration to read, however hard I tried. My mind was all over the place. But drawing I could do. It helped me focus on something outside myself. I listened to every record he owned, ones I'd never seen or heard before. It was a way of keeping him close. I found a record of Romanian folk dances buried at the back of the crate one morning. I had no idea where it could've come from, but the music was strange and beautiful and full of mournful Gypsy wailings and rhythms that made me think I was listening to coded messages from beyond.

Two months later I started dating one of the other teachers in the volunteer program. She was older, twenty-nine, from La Plata, Argentina, and taught Spanish. Marina had short red hair and enjoyed a reputation around the department as being a pleasant and dedicated teacher. I'd been interested in her from the moment we met. She had a pretty face and smile and always moved her hips with a lovely feminine rolling motion when I saw her walking between the staff room and her class. I'd catch up with her and flirt, making it clear I was interested but not desperate. We'd been on friendly terms since I started volunteering, but it took me a while to decide if her pleasant nature was natural and unprompted or had something to do with me or if she'd made some conscious decision that a winning attitude would serve her well in a new city.

After we started sleeping together, she asked if I'd ever lost anyone close to me. I didn't tell her about my parents, only about Miles. We were in bed, shoulder to shoulder, staring up at the ceiling.

"Your best friend?" she said.

"Yes."

She didn't say if she'd lost anyone herself, though I suspected she had. Sometimes she'd curl into me and talk in Spanish—a language I didn't understand then—for as long as an hour. Maybe she wanted to introduce me to the sound of it, or to express things to herself that she couldn't in English, despite her fluency in it. I had no idea what she was saying to me, of course. For all I knew she could have been talking about afternoon picnics with her family back in La Plata. There might have been a more sinister bent to these stories, I couldn't tell. The disappearances, death squads, a family with a military secret, perhaps. I was beginning to read about these terrible histories in the newspapers. But if such stories touched her directly, I never knew. I felt like I'd stepped outside of my world for a short time when I was with her, though, and the sadness felt different, still there but somehow altered, and I was almost happy.

I spent many hours at her apartment that spring. She shared a flat with a roommate just twenty minutes from where Holly lived. On Fridays I met her at the high school after work and walked her home. I found out later she had more than one lover, that her kind nature was not reserved strictly for me. This thought didn't bother me. We spent most of our time together in her bed. But one afternoon I brought her back to my pullout couch.

"These are very strange," she said, leafing through one of my sketch pads naked, her knees raised against her chest. "What do you call these things in English?"

"Doodles."

"You doodle. I like your doodles. English is a funny language."

"Yes," I said, "it is."

One evening I went down to the basement and piled my books of drawings into the furnace, then sat with the superintendent and watched them burn. He was an old Italian fellow with a big, round head and thin arms. He wore a white muscle shirt while he tinkered away at the building's pipes and mysterious inner workings. I had a vague understanding that his wife had died some years before Holly and Miles arrived here and that he'd taken over from the previous super, who according to tenant lore had experienced some trouble with the law and was forcefully removed from his flat on the fourth floor. He was broad-shouldered and didn't say much, this new man, and sat peacefully on a small paint-splattered chair beside his workbench, his platter-sized hands resting in his lap, while my graphite cartoon drawings went up in smoke.

The outdoor terraces on Saint-Denis opened again, and on a fine night sometime in early summer I stepped out onto the fire escape to enjoy the first pleasant evening after a week of rain. I climbed up to the roof of our building and found Holly alone, scooping soil into a five-gallon pail from a large burlap sack. I hadn't seen her in days. At least twenty of these pails were gathered around her like a brood of children, and in each was a small circular garden. I took this in for a moment, my heart sinking, then started back down the stairs. But when she called my name I stopped, took a deep breath and turned around. "You're busy," I said, walking toward her over the flat tarry surface. Her hands were stained the color of the soil she'd been turning.

"It's quiet up here," she said. "It helps me think."

"You've got a nice view, anyway."

"We'll eventually be able to do something with these tomatoes, once they come up," she said. "The super grows them. You've met him, right? He's from Verona or somewhere like that. I've been helping out a bit up here."

I watched her for a moment without saying anything.

Then she said, "You really like her, don't you?"

"Marina? Yes."

There was another silence.

"I miss him," she said.

"Me, too."

"I've been horrible to you. I know that now. I've been horrible. I guess I got lost."

"It hasn't been the greatest year," I said.

"Don't ever let me do that to you again, okay?"

I didn't say anything. I felt like crying. I felt like calling her a selfish fucking cunt. But I knew as I stood there that I'd been as bad or worse. The city lay before us under a blue dome of sky, and over the rooftops and the distant cap of trees a great cloud the size of a mountain rolled upward and split into fractals of brilliant color.

"It's been harder than I ever could've imagined," she said.

I felt my heart bursting in two directions. This was the first time we'd mentioned Miles since he'd died, so now the emotions came rushing in. I felt like screaming or jumping off the roof, but I was also jubilant. This was the sort of acknowledgment I'd been waiting to hear for years from my brother, that he'd been wounded, as I had been, or that he felt something true and deep about our parents. He still hadn't said anything of the sort, but here was a glimpse into Holly's heart. It was as simple as that—the softness in her voice, this small sign of contrition and connection. Suddenly our grief was pulling us together, not tearing us apart.

"There's going to be lots of tomatoes this year," she said, wiping her hands. "They won't be ready till the end of the summer, though."

"I don't know anything about tomatoes," I said, stepping forward and kissing her on the mouth.

She just stared at me, speechless.

"You don't need to be in love with me," I said. "You don't need to say anything."

She turned and walked to the far side of the roof, where the evening was being swallowed and burned up by the city lights. I went back downstairs, thinking I'd just ruined everything, and when she entered the apartment an hour later, she pretended nothing had happened.

In August we picked and ate those tomatoes and felt their sun-warmed juices running down our forearms. We started spending time together. We carried a hibachi and two lawn chairs up there and often opened a bottle of wine and ate something and sat and talked for hours and watched the light change over the city. It's difficult now to recall the conversations we had, or how much time we actually spent talking, but the weather was good, and I remember watching the flickering lights and believing that our lives had finally been allowed to begin. I hadn't kissed her a second time, nor had she responded one way or another to my declaration that she didn't have to love me back. In the months that passed we never spoke about it. Each night after we came back downstairs, I pulled out the couch, stretched out and waited for the sound of the bedroom door to creak and the footsteps and the rush of pleasure as she slipped into my bed. But her door never opened.

If Holly had an opinion about Marina, she didn't share it with me. I was still seeing her but my heart wasn't in it anymore. I stayed with her once a week and on a rare occasion, when Holly was off at her classes, she'd come home with me for an hour or two. One afternoon the phone rang. Marina was standing in the living room pulling her underwear back on, and she picked up the phone and said, "Bonjour, L'Académie de Montréal." If it was pure reflex or an attempt at humor I don't know. We burst out laughing, then I took the phone from her and said hello.

When the other end remained silent I knew it was Holly. Later that night I tried to read but wasn't able to focus. My mind was going a million miles an hour.

Holly emerged from her bedroom and sat down on the sofa beside me, tucking her knees up into her chest. "You don't even care about her," she said. "I don't understand you."

I closed my book and slipped it between the cushions. "Probably not in the way you mean, anyway," I said.

"What other way is there?"

"I feel good with her," I said. "That counts for something."

"You two can do that at her place. Please, not here. You've got your life, I know that. But please don't do that here."

"We usually don't," I said.

She looked around the apartment. It had changed little since I'd first sat here almost three years before.

"I have this strange feeling all the time," she said. "You know when you do something and there's only part of you that's doing it? And the other part of you is watching it happen? You know that feeling?"

"I think so."

"It's like you're trapped in a room of mirrors. Does that make any sense? Or am I just losing my mind?" She smiled a heartbroken, confused smile.

"I don't think you're losing your mind."

"I hope getting old doesn't mean being this fucked up the rest of your life."

"I'm pretty sure it doesn't," I said.

"Who I used to be, I think about that person now. I was such a kid. I can't stand thinking about her."

"I thought she was nice," I said. "She was smart. I liked listening to her talk. You made me think about things I'd never really thought about before I met you."

"I guess I should've learned something from reading all those stupid German novels."

"Last winter was pretty horrible," I said.

"I'm tired of feeling like shit. That's one thing I'm sure of." She looked around the apartment again, then stared at her hands for what seemed like a long time.

"I'm probably the most aware person there ever was. I'm not complimenting myself, believe me. It's something I hate—being aware of everything you do at all times isn't exactly a party."

"I'll bet," I said.

"My mind's always going. Maybe I'm just a big fat solipsist or something. I don't know if you understand what I'm talking about."

"I think we all are in some way."

"I haven't known anything else since Miles died. And then today happens. I guess I felt shock. For the first time in so long it was just me, and I wasn't just thinking about how sad I was. I wasn't watching myself being miserable. You know what it was that did it?"

"I'd like to know," I said.

"It was that laughing on the other end of the line. How it made me feel. I heard your voice laughing at me."

"I feel terrible about that."

"I know you do. But that's not why I'm telling you this. I'm telling you this because that laughing made me jealous. It made me think about us." She looked up at me. "I guess that's surprising to you."

"It is, a bit," I said.

She leaned forward and kissed me, and in a flash of heat the greyness inside me disappeared.

Every fiber in my body pounded with hope for the future. Feeling my spirits lift, I touched her cheek. She didn't stop my hands when I tried to open her shirt and jeans. We made love on the floor beside that couch I'd been sleeping on, where I'd dreamed of her, and then

I lifted her into my arms and carried her into her bedroom and made love to her again. My heart filled with joy. I had thought about making love to Holly hundreds of times, what she would look like naked, what we would do together, if she would do certain things that I asked her, but my fantasies were nothing compared with the perfect intimacy we felt together.

In the middle of the night she left the bed. Sleeping lightly, I reached over and found her side was empty. I heard the bathroom door close. A minute later the toilet flushed, but she didn't come back.

"Are you okay?" I said, standing outside the bathroom door feeling confused and tired but still exhilarated. What we'd just done had solved everything, I thought. Clarified everything. Put everything else behind us. What we'd shared was natural and perfect and beautiful. When I'd held her in my arms, I knew nothing better had ever happened in my life, yet now I felt worried and full of regret. I pushed the door open. She was sitting on the edge of the tub, still naked, holding her hands to her face.

"What's the matter?" I said.

"I don't know. I just don't know what's happening to me."

Holly took me back into her bed the following night. Trembling with excitement, we made love with even more intensity than we had the evening before. But afterward the same melancholy took hold. She became distant, worried, then apologetic. It wasn't as bad and didn't last as long this time. Still, it was terrible to watch. She was in pain, and I didn't know how to fix it. I couldn't understand how something as great as what we did and felt together could cause her to roll back into herself like this.

The fear and depression that overtook her after we made love seemed to diminish as time went on. I thought she was beating whatever it was that plagued her. Then one night I woke up in the dark, and again I was alone in bed. The covers were torn up, her pillow on the floor. She was in the living room sitting in front of the turntable wearing a pair of headphones. The room was completely dark but for the pale blue glow of the stereo lights playing on the side of her face, her head bobbing slightly to something I couldn't hear. I wondered then what it must have felt like to be loved as deeply as she had loved Miles.

It happened again the next night, and then the night after that. It became a regular occurrence, a ghostly ritual. I'd wake up and feel the empty space beside me. I'd stand in the bedroom doorway and watch her listening to music in the dark. Finally I lost count of how many times I saw this. I never interrupted her. I knew she was with him, thinking of him, trying to bring him back. In the morning it was always the Waterboys record sitting on the turntable, the one we'd been listening to the night Miles died. He was still here in that apartment with us. It took finding Holly out there every night for me to really understand that.

. . .

That we were still together, in some fashion, more than a year after his death, and possibly had a shot at being happy and sharing a life—wasn't that hopeful, and even what he might have wanted? Nothing we did could be ugly or disrespectful. We were the two people he loved most. I didn't think he'd want to take the chance of happiness away from us. It took a few months, but eventually we were able to lie in bed together after making love and talk about ourselves as a couple without feeling the world was about to crash down on our heads.

Miles's name didn't come up when Holly first started talking about going abroad for her master's thesis. She saw opportunities in West Germany. We both knew we would always associate Montreal with our friend's death. The thought of leaving grew stronger as we both began to see that this city would always hold that memory. He was everywhere we looked, in the streets, the cafés, in that small apartment the three of us had shared. He was a shadow we needed to outrun.

At night when I got home from teaching, I'd find Holly reading and curled up on the couch in her pajamas, with a pencil and an open notepad on the coffee table. As I threw together something to eat she'd read aloud in German. I understood nothing at all of that language, but I listened, in love with her voice and the expressions that moved over her face, and often wondered when the time would come when our friend would finally move off and leave us alone together.

. . .

We flew to West Berlin in the fall of 1987 and lived in a small apartment on the fourth floor of a five-story walk-up. The window in our living room looked down on the narrow street. There was a student bar down there, and every morning I saw a little round lady in a blue frock and Adidas running shoes sweeping the sidewalk out front. We went in there at night and watched the crowds of students and drank beer from enormous bottles. At each table there seemed to be a subject of great importance under discussion. The young men wore Palestinian scarves wrapped around their necks and smoked hand-rolled cigarettes and handed around flyers that called attention to their favorite causes.

Finally, after a few weeks, we were waved over to join one of these roundtables and provide the North American perspective. Eager faces leaned forward, but I had no positions or arguments on the matters at hand. I couldn't talk about the arms race. I held no firm notions on the Sandinistas or the PLO or the Solidarity Movement in Poland's dockyards. I was unable to stake a claim on one side or the other. It wasn't indifference that bogged me down but an appreciation of the baffling complexity. Always present in my mind, if never clearly discernible, were the strands of truth and the limitless contingencies that spun out from the centre of whatever issue lay before us. At the heart of certainty there was danger, ideology, blindness. One evening I attempted to share this interpretation with three students who quickly pointed out the moral

cowardice of such an approach and drew parallels to
Swiss neutrality and the complacency of the German
citizenry in the lead-up to the war. I tried to articulate
my position but was not invited to participate again.

Holly spent her days up at the university working
on her thesis. Her adviser was a serious old gentleman
from Dresden named Schreiber, who taught a course on
modern German philosophy. She introduced us on a
foggy afternoon in November.

"You are an English teacher at a record company
here?" he said.

"That's right," I said.

A few weeks after we arrived, I'd been taken on by
a small language academy that had contracts with a
number of large corporations. One of them was a mul-
tinational recording company. After two weeks one of
my students, the ranking executive, pulled me aside
and proposed that we dump the middleman. He paid
less money, and I made more.

"And do you like Berlin?" Holly's professor asked.
His bottom lip was quivering slightly, and he held a
battered old briefcase in his right hand. He was probably close to seventy years old.

"It's an exciting city," I said. "Sure, I do."

"Berlin is the new Galápagos," he said. "It is an
island populated by a fascinating new species of German."

I fell in love with the way Germans spoke to me
in my own tongue. There was an almost total absence
of idioms and clichés in the English I heard there,
and they couldn't rely on partially formed thoughts

or vaguely expressed ideas like native speakers could. I'd noticed this at the bars and parties Holly and I went to when our nights ended in conversation about the Wall or the Green Party or Ronald Reagan, and I found myself as dazzled by the clarity of their expressions as I was hesitant to accept the absolutism of their declarations.

I went to the record company four days a week and spent most of the three hours I billed them for daily talking with my students' secretaries. The executives were hardly ever around. I read magazines and newspapers and sipped from my bottle of Spezi until one of them waved me into his office to walk him through some phrasal verbs until something more interesting came up. The one who needed the most help was a Parisian named Marcel, and as outsiders we enjoyed pointing out to each other the peculiarities of the Germanic character.

Rolf, the man who had hired me, was forty-seven years old and liked to gaze out his office window and watch the parking lot below as he talked to me, in English, about his life. He was married and had two children, but that didn't stop him from sleeping with prostitutes as often as he could. He told me this without compunction, as though it were the most natural thing in the world. I didn't share my prostitute story, which was nothing I was proud of. When I thought back on that night, I felt uncomfortable and awkward that I'd stupidly let myself get pulled into a situation where I felt obligated, even pressured, to play along. Rolf, though, was proud of the number of hookers he'd had sex with. He traveled once or twice a month and came home with stories of call girls crawling all over him at the Regency or the Groucho Club or some anonymous Marriott. He was a short man with silver hair and spoke explicitly about the sexual acts he'd performed on his most recent trip, whether to Hamburg, New York or Amsterdam. He didn't recount these stories with any sense of titillation or sexual energy as far as I could tell, more like a frat boy bragging about the number of goldfish he'd managed to swallow live.

When I wasn't sitting with one of my three execs or chatting up the secretaries, I claimed a cafeteria table by the windows on the second floor and took a stumbling swing at learning a bit of German. Most of the people I worked with spoke English well enough that I didn't have to extend myself, but the staff here was different. They had very little English, so to this day my best German is located in the practical nouns and verbs used in a cafeteria. When not engaged in halting conversations, I'd sit there and watch the attendant in a small glass-and-aluminum station at the far end of the parking lot or read or sketch something, all the while thinking that trying to learn a new language was like climbing up a mountain into a rock slide.

The parking attendant was a Turkish fellow named Gorkhan, whose German seemed to be very good. He'd been in the country for sixteen years, raising and lowering the red-and-white barrier that blocked traffic access to all but paid employees and registered visitors. A man trapped in a glass box all day long these days will spend his shift talking on a cell phone, but not then. Gorkhan was an island. He referred to his out-post as Checkpoint Charlie.

One night I woke up and saw Holly standing at our bedroom window holding a piece of paper in her hand, a letter, I thought. In the morning I found it under her pillow. It was the Ezra Pound poem Miles had taped up on the living room wall back in Montreal. That's when I began to understand she could never leave that place—not with my presence constantly reminding her of what we'd both lost. I was the problem. With me at her side she could never break the pattern of her grieving. Whenever she looked at me, she remembered our friend and the life they'd had together. I think I knew what I needed to do well before admitting it to myself. What it meant horrified me. I did all I could to push it aside, to wait, to come up with excuses. But I was always drawn back to the same conclusion. I had to leave. I was in love with Holly and knew I would be forever. But that love would never be as strong as the sadness that ruled her.

We were standing in front of the Brandenburg Gate when I told her I had to leave. But I didn't give her the real reason. I was restless, I said. I was just going through something.

"You're a strange boy," she said.

A light snow was falling around us, the flakes melt-ing in her hair and against her face.

"Sicily, maybe. Or Morocco."

"My head's all over the place, but you know I love you," she said. "You know I want to be with you."

"I know," I said.

"Maybe Tunisia. I'd go to Tunisia if I were you."

"Okay. I'll go there."

"And when you come back, I'd marry me if I were you."

"I'd marry you, too," I said.

"Tunisia."

"I don't even know what language they speak there."

"Tunisian?" she said.

"It's probably as good a place as any to dig up those essential moral dictates in life."

She pinched my arm and smiled. "I'm never going to live that one down, am I?"

The Kantian philosophy she'd rolled out for me at the Montreal diner was still something I teased her about every once in a while. But it was also something that had started to make a lot of sense to me.

I put my hands on her face and kissed her. "I'll probably be back in no time," I said.

⇥ Six

It was a cowardly way of ending it.
I didn't tell her I could never come back, since I could
hardly believe it myself. So there she waited while I
stepped into the current of life and was swept away
from her until we met again that day years later in
Toronto. I thought about her each and every day but
didn't call her. That was the hell of it. I was the problem, and the farther away I kept myself, the better off
she'd be. My love for Holly itself became the shadow
we needed to outrun.

It was mid-March 1988, the days short and cold
and miserable. I spent time in Amsterdam and Paris
writing postcards I didn't send, drank a lot of cheap
wine and finally moved along through a series of small
Dutch towns. In one of them I met a med student
in a bar who said he was leaving for the Costa Brava,
where he'd cram for finals with friends for ten days.
He said he had room for a passenger if I helped him
out with gas money. The next morning we met in the
town square, with his car loaded for the trip. We talked
nonstop as we drove. I was in love with a girl who
could never be happy with me, I told him, because I
reminded her of a sad time in her life. Near the end
of our trip he asked where I was staying. The plan was

to sleep rough in a bus station or park, I said, since that's what I'd been doing for weeks. He told me I'd get robbed if I didn't get killed first.

I stayed on the coast for a few days in a villa owned by the parents of one of the girls studying there that week. I didn't bother anyone during the day, just wandered around the village, tried to read and looked at the sea. Everything I saw brought Holly to mind. I hadn't spoken to her since I left, though I'd finally posted a card telling her I was fine. I didn't tell her where I was or what my plans were. I didn't have any. A small library of books had been left behind by various people who'd rented the villa over the years. Most were in German, but there was also a shelf of English novels and poetry and translations. From eight in the morning to three in the afternoon the place was deathly quiet. I sat in a lounge chair overlooking the Catalan hills and discovered Herman Hesse, whose writing reminded me of the torment of my own soul. He understood. I could practically feel his hand reaching up through the page. If someone else could know and write so well about what I was feeling, I wasn't losing my mind after all. Suffering from the widest, deepest heartache I'd ever known, I almost turned around and headed back to her. But I knew what I carried in my heart for Holly was the very thing that was destroying her.

After a few nights at the villa I hitched west across the northern coast of Spain and landed in a small city called Santander. I rented a room in a drafty flat in the centre of town, a fifteen-minute walk from the ocean. The flat's owner, the Señora, was a nurse. When she wasn't at the hospital working the night shift, she sat in the darkness of her small kitchen smoking and turning over cards in a perpetual game of solitaire. She was raising a son on her own, a boy named Baldomero, and while fully employed still had to take in the occasional renter to help get her through to the end of the month. She was an attractive woman, and in her early thirties, I guessed, but a sense of greyness and gloom hung over her. Her floors smelled of bleach. Her younger sister, an equally distracted woman, lived on the same floor at the end of the hall, and she prepared her nephew's evening meal and made sure he got to bed on time.

I'd told the Señora that I was studying at one of the city's language academies, but I wasn't a student anywhere anymore. I'd given that up in Montreal. Now I spent my days walking the streets and looking for cheap places to eat and wondering if leaving Holly had been the right thing to do. Could I be sure I'd been the cause of the melancholy that drew her down into those depths?

Baldomero, who was twelve years old, occupied the room next to mine. I didn't know who had previously occupied my room or, for that matter, where the boy's father was. Sometimes in the early morning I heard the Señora come in from her shift and make herself a cup of tea and then the creaking of her son's bedsprings when she lay down beside him to wake him for school.

Instead of a wintery Berlin view, my window looked over the city's main boulevard, a long pedestrian walkway lined with palm trees and booths and tables sheltered from the weather by makeshift coverings of blue tarp or clear plastic. Sometimes I watched for Holly from that window, as if she'd come to tell me that the pain she felt was worth it, that she could endure anything as long as she was with me. Wasn't this the price of love? In a moment of weakness I sent a postcard telling her where I was, with no mention of when I might return.

It rained almost every day. But whenever it softened to a drizzle or stopped altogether, the vendors suddenly appeared with their cages of rabbits and canaries or pails of carnations, and the crowds streamed down the avenue, and the town seemed alive and bright with springtime. I left the flat early most mornings and explored the city. I found the port straight off and followed the coast for three or four hours, then doubled back. The next day I went down to the train station and watched the African men selling transistor radios and pirated cassette tapes and small wooden giraffes and elephants. Their skin as black as ink under those cloudy Atlantic skies, they seemed to vanish into thin air when the municipal police showed up. And then they reappeared only minutes later, unloaded their wares and once again turned to selling.

I found a decent library with a good English-language selection and read Aldous Huxley, Arthur Koestler and a hardcover copy of *For Whom the Bell Tolls*. I'd read it before but I took it down off the shelf and again was thrilled to imagine the pine forests in the sierra north of Madrid. It had seemed romantic and dangerous, and I realized it had been part of the reason I'd crossed the border into Spain. I wasn't allowed to sign these books out without a library card, which wasn't available without proper Spanish documentation, but the library was warm and dry, and the window I sat beside had a clear view of a park and a hill covered in trees that was sometimes shrouded in a foggy Atlantic mist.

A few weeks after my arrival I met a girl named Carmen in the student ghetto. She was standing with another girl at the bar in El Mago, a place I'd been going to over the last few days. On the brick wall behind them were large posters featuring a bullfight, the Stones and a black-and-white shot of Miles Davis cradling his trumpet. I liked the music playing in the bar that night. I can't recall what it was, but it was loud, and everyone was talking and arguing and stubbing out cigarettes on the stone floor. I was alone most of the day and going crazy to meet people. I'd never been so lonely and had prowled up and down this street night after night hoping to meet someone I could talk to. I was looking at that beautiful Miles Davis portrait, almost waiting for him to look up and smile, when Carmen and Arantxa noticed me. I screwed up my courage and walked over and introduced myself.

"You like jazz?" Carmen asked in Spanish.

For half a second I was flattered. Maybe that meant I looked the part. "Not really," I told her in English. "I just like the look of that photograph."

Carmen was the pretty one, though she was self-conscious about how receded her teeth were. She tried to cover this up by quickly drawing her upper lip down over her teeth when she smiled or laughed, which she did enough that you could tell she was a kind and happy person who liked to have a good time. But it was precisely her mouth that made her attractive to me. They asked me lots of questions that night— what it was like where I came from, what I liked about Spain, where I was going next. It was the first conversation I'd had in weeks.

By then I'd very nearly gone through the money I'd earned at the record company. I only ate one meal a day, usually at Casa Mariano, the cheapest dive I could find. It had wooden beams and sawdust on the floor and included a half liter of wine with every dish, though I never touched it. Given that Holly was always on my mind, I didn't need the gloominess of spirit that came with drinking wine in the middle of the day.

After lunch I would walk down to the harbor to where the car ferry docked, the biggest ship I'd ever seen. I was happy to sit there for hours, thinking about Holly or the pretty girl I'd met at El Mago, and listen to the English passengers as they came off the ship.

In the late afternoons, back in the flat, I heard the Señora and her sister talking in the kitchen. Neither of them looked up when I came in, and I did my best to disappear into my room. On the one or two occasions I'd sat in the living room with the landlady and her son, I looked at the photograph in an antique silver frame of a young man holding a child in his arms— Baldomero and his father, I thought. I didn't know if he'd died or run off, and it wasn't my place to ask. But I remember him as ordinary looking, a little dull and heavy, with sullen eyes. He had dark eyebrows and the solid round face I grew accustomed to later in the north of Spain, and the tired expression about his eyes you can see everywhere else.

Carmen, Arantxa and I began to meet regularly, usually at night, and I looked forward to these evenings all day. When I saw their familiar shapes walking toward me in the evening's misting rain, the promise of some small connection with this place appeared along with them, and the girls would wave and I'd rehearse my greetings and wonder what it would be like to kiss this shy and beautiful girl.

They both liked to talk about Spanish boys. According to Carmen, they were selfish and arrogant and thought a girl owed them everything. Arantxa said they were raised by their mothers to be utterly dependent on women. Neither of these girls wanted anything to do with them. Carmen was studying French and German at university, and Arantxa was in her last months of secretarial college. I remember thinking that their lives were far better thought out and organized than mine. Carmen was usually nervous and giddy, speaking quickly and always punctuating her questions with a negative, as if preparing herself for some inevitable reversal. *You had a good day, no? People from your country are very serious, no?* She had straight brown hair, pale

skin and a strong, perfect nose. She was always smiling, unlike her friend, who talked about moving to
Germany after she graduated.

   Late one afternoon I saw Arantxa buying a canary
from a birdman on the Paseo Menéndez Pelayo, just a
block or so down from my flat. The air was heavy with
mist that day, and I was heading home after struggling
at the library for most of the day to write a letter—the
only one I ever sent to Holly. I'd finally gathered the
courage to explain why I'd left her. Meanwhile, she'd
sent four or five by then, in each of which she mentioned coming to see me and asked how things were
and if Spain was as wonderful as she imagined. Could I
write soon? Is everything okay? She wrote her letters by
hand in blue ink in the perfect script I knew well. These
were beautiful physical artifacts, long and detailed and
written at different points in her day or night. *About
to head into class now, more later . . .* And she'd start up
again, *Just released from a Kafka lecture . . .* She ended
each letter with a line or two from whatever she was
reading at the time. I couldn't help remembering that
Pound poem on the wall in Montreal.

   I was thinking about the letter I'd just posted,
rewriting parts of it or tearing it up completely in my
head, when I saw a grey-haired man reach his arm out
and hand Arantxa the bird, its small yellow head sticking out from between his fingers. I stopped walking
and watched her, waiting for the moment when she'd
set the creature free. What else could she do with it?
She'd never shown an interest in birds or anything else,
for that matter, other than escaping this rainy port

town. But I saw her turn away, and she disappeared into the crowds on the boulevard.

I walked over to the student ghetto and stayed till after midnight. I was feeling miserable. All I could see now in my mind's eye was Holly ripping open that envelope and reading the letter I'd sent. Now I didn't know if I'd done the right thing.

When I got home hours later, I found the Señora watching TV in the living room.

"Hola," I said. "Good night."

"Good night. Wait."

"Yes?"

"Look at me. What do you see?"

"I don't understand," I said.

"A nurse of fourteen years. That's what you see. They've thrown me to the street. That's how this country is now."

"I'm sorry," I said. "That's terrible." I stood there for a moment longer, not knowing what else to say. "But you'll find something, right? Sure you will. People always need nurses."

"What this country needs is another Franco," she said. "We need a strong man. People like me are thrown into the street. It's the cowards who ruin everything. Cowards who do what they're told and not what's right."

A knock on my door brought me up out of a shallow sleep sometime later that night. Without moving I looked at my watch sitting on the night table. The knob turned slightly and the door pushed open and a sliver of light reached across my bed. A deep silence filled the room. My heart was crashing in my chest. Then the door was closed, and a moment later I heard the sofa springs creak in the living room, and all was quiet.

After a few hours at the library the next day I carried a sandwich up to the zoo and ate it sitting on a bench under a plane tree. It was the first sunny afternoon in a week. Without thinking too deeply about my land-lady's situation, I finished my sandwich and sat back and felt the sun on my face, then walked around the zoo and looked at the animals. When I came to the polar bears, I leaned against the safety support and looked down and watched them. There were just two of them. Their pen was comprised mostly of natural rock, built right into the cliff. They had access to a small strip of sand, and the water that rushed in and out of the space they patrolled came directly from the ocean.

I met Carmen later that evening and walked the length of the harbor with her five or six times. The water was calm, the air still, and the doleful sound of a Spanish guitar came from an unseen radio. We went to a bar we knew nearby and had a drink. It started to rain as I walked her back to her apartment, and she stopped and looked at me.

"*Me gustas,*" she said. "I like you. You're very differ-ent from the Spanish boys."

"I guess I always will be."

"Maybe that's the reason you left where you're from in the first place, no?"

I told her she was probably right.

"So you will stay for a little while?"

"Sure, I will," I said. "It rains too much here but otherwise I like it. The ocean is beautiful."

We were holding hands now, and I kissed her and said I'd like to see Santander in the summertime when the beach was full of happy splashing families and girls in bikinis. She pinched me and smiled, just like Holly had done six or seven weeks earlier, and told me maybe I wasn't so different from all the Spanish boys after all.

"I guess you'll just have to wait and see," I said.

Baldomero was already in bed when I got home. I'd walked Carmen back to her front step, and now I found the Señora flipping through a magazine at the kitchen table. She didn't say hello or even look up. I went into my room and shut the door behind me and undressed and got into bed and thought about Carmen and what Santander would look like in a few months' time. And then I thought about Holly and that excitement vanished, leaving me as blue as I'd ever felt. I listened to the rain begin and calculated in my head how much money I had spent that day. At least this might keep me from thinking about girls.

Still distracted, I got up and sat down at the writing desk that looked out over the rainy boulevard and opened the top drawer where I kept my traveler's checks pressed between the pages of a Spanish-English dictionary. The book was there, but the checks were not. I walked out to the kitchen and told the Señora that someone had taken money from my room.

"That is not possible," she said. "No one goes in there." She flipped a page of her magazine.

I told her I needed my money back.

"I am no thief," she said. "In the streets there are thieves. Not in this house."

"All my money was in that desk."

"You will pay what you owe and then you will leave."

I went into my room and wondered if it was possible I'd made some mistake. Had I moved the checks without remembering? But there could be no doubt. The money had been stolen. I waited, wondering what to do, then just before dawn I packed my bag in the dark and quietly walked through the apartment. The Señora's door was shut tight. I pressed an ear against the door and listened, then took the photograph of the boy and his father from the mantel and slipped it into my backpack. I found her wallet in her purse hanging on a hook by the front door. It didn't contain much, but I took it all.

The rain had stopped falling now, and the air was cold and damp, and the streets were still empty. I walked to Carmen's apartment and stood on the street watching the windows on the third floor. I didn't know which window was hers, but they were all dark.

At the train station I found the group of Africans waiting beside the kiosk. I removed the picture and dropped it in the trash bin and showed them the frame.

They passed it among themselves, shaking their

heads as if this was the poorest imitation of silver they'd ever seen. "No, hombre, no," one of them said, shrugging. Finally the guy selling pirated tapes offered me my pick of ten cassettes as a fair trade. I told them I needed pesetas. They conferred again, passing the frame around, and in the end I sold it for one thousand pesetas, barely ten dollars. Though it was worth much more, they pretended they were doing me a kindness. I bought a ticket on the first train out of there.

⇥ Seven

On a windy October afternoon in 2005 I asked Hilary if she'd like a tour of the new academy. Hilary was the woman I'd interrupted at the coffee shop after speaking with the Sikh business owner earlier that fall. She was sitting under the Picasso print in the Starbucks on Yonge Street, sipping a latte. "You've been listening to that racket for weeks," I said. "What do you say?" The hammering and banging had been going on a lot longer than that, in fact, and things had warmed up between us considerably since our first meeting.

"It sounds like a war zone up there," she said, drawing a strand of hair behind her ear.

I walked her through the maze of sawhorses and vats of plaster and extension cords. The classrooms were framed in at that point, and the drywall was going up. You now could get a good sense of what the whole place would look like in a few weeks.

"It's a helluva project," she said.

I showed her my office and the view looking down over College Street.

"Boss gets the best sight lines, I see," she said.

"Wouldn't have it any other way."

I toured her through the rest of the place, then

locked up, and we strolled down to the Elephant &
Castle for a drink and a basket of nachos. She was a
Guinness drinker, she said—had been ever since a trip
to Dublin a few years back.

"Fabulous place. I'm there twice a year, for a while
now."

"I suppose you have an academy there, too?"

I tilted my head and shrugged.

"Well, well. Mr. Big Shot," she said. "What other
plans for conquering the world should I know about?"

We ended up going home together that night, and
soon after that we fell into a comfortable routine. I
got the impression that she was as lonely as I was. She
camouflaged this fact with a number of pressing needs:
to get her book of essays ready for publication and to
bail out of the continuing-studies program where she'd
been teaching for too long—contract work, a "ghetto"
as far as she was concerned—and find a full-time fac-
ulty job at a university. I learned over the weeks that
followed about the boy named Hans she'd fallen in
love with in high school. He became a police officer
after they married and got to telling her stories about
injecting urine into oranges as a practical joke around
the station house, as if she'd see the humor in that. It
was scary they let a guy like him carry a gun, she said.
She'd married him at the age of eighteen, three months
after graduating, then walked out on him the day she
turned twenty-three. She'd never make a mistake like
that again, she told me.

"Marrying a cop, you mean?" I asked.

"Marrying, period," she said.

After she ditched Hans, she went to India on one of those soul-searching missions we all hear about. The difference is, this trip amounted to something. She joined up with an NGO in Delhi, where she stayed for three years. She'd never seen anything like it, she said.

"The slums?" I said.

"The slums were horrible, but that's not what I'm talking about. It's the competition between the NGOs there. Before long it was obvious we were stabbing one another in the back trying to get the same job done, always fighting for funding and turf. I thought that's just how India was. After that I came back here and got my undergraduate degree, then my master's. But I was still thinking about it six years later, so off I went again. This time to the Philippines. I loved it, though it was the same thing there, fighting over every dollar and patch of ground just like in India. The survival instincts of most of those NGOs are the same. The ones I know, anyway. They almost forget what they're doing it for. It's like an end in itself, keeping the machine alive."

I admired her determination and the idealism she kept imperfectly hidden beneath her hardened sense of life's depressing fiascoes. She had a desk at a ten-member writing co-op on Ossington. She cycled out there most days when she wasn't teaching and pored through her research and inched her essays toward completion. I read one of them, and it was incredibly complicated, full of charts and graphs meant to elucidate theses that remained intangible to me. I had a strong head for business but didn't understand much at all about this. I was sure she'd end up at Princeton.

That fall and winter she spent most Friday nights at my place. We'd meet at the coffee shop after work and cycle east into Little Chinatown, pick up some seafood and end up rolling around on my living room couch, then put supper together as she explained the big economic ideas she'd been hacking away at that day. I'd try to make a connection with something I'd learned in putting my language schools together, and she'd listen politely and maybe nod and say, "Yeah, that's right, something along those lines," but I always felt she thought the actual giving and taking of money somehow sullied the purity of the models she was interested in.

She also liked to talk about her friends, especially the three who'd been there for her at the end of her relationship with Hans. She was exceptionally devoted to these women, two of whom I met later that fall at a salsa club on College Street. I hadn't been thrilled about the prospect of going to a club but felt, ridiculously I see now, that it might be something a man in my position—that is, one who was sleeping with a younger woman—was supposed to do. It wasn't all that bad, though I'm sure I made a spectacle of myself. Paula and Danielle spent the night walking me through the dance steps they'd spin off and demonstrate, coming in and out like a yo-yo on a string, putting their lovely sweaty arms around me. "You lived in Madrid for how long?" Danielle said, shouting above the music. I tried to convince them that Madrid had nothing to do with salsa, but they didn't believe me.

A few hours later that night, Hilary sat half dressed and staring out my bedroom window over the neighborhood. A light rain had started to fall. "You know something funny?" she said.

"Tell me."

"We never fought, Hans and I. I don't think we argued once. I just started to see that he wasn't what I wanted. It wasn't my life. Can you believe that?"

"Sure I can."

"I used to feel this incredible admiration. I was so in love I could taste it. I would have eaten glass for that man. And then I just didn't care anymore." She paused, staring out the dark window. "He didn't change one bit. He didn't do anything different. It was me."

"First love," I said.

"Maybe that's our only true love. I don't know, but I sometimes think so. Maybe everything after that's just us trying to find what we've lost." She looked at me with a sad half smile. "Maybe that's too depressing to admit. I hope you don't mind my saying so."

I knew what she was getting at. She was talking about that hope you feel before the first heartbreak or betrayal or the first signs of your own limitations come into view. When your heart knows only the perfect impulse to share everything with someone without shame or resignation or restraint. She was talking about the difference between who we used to be and who we were now and how the space that remains when love ends becomes an empty grey thing you never thought you'd become.

My spirits began to rise as the holiday season approached. I was due to go home for Christmas. I hadn't seen Ava since coming back to Toronto, though we usually spoke once or twice a week. One snowy evening I inked nine green stars in the corresponding squares of the calendar hanging on my kitchen wall. Each symbolized a full day I'd spend with my daughter in Madrid.

The week before my departure Nate and I took the boys up to the cottage pictured in the handsome coffee-table book he'd pulled out for me my first day here. Though it was smaller in real life, it was all rustic charm and exposed rafters and bunk beds, everything you'd hope for in a place on a lake. There was a big stone fireplace, which we stoked up as soon as we pulled in, and from the windows you could see the lake and the evergreens on the far shore. In the afternoon we shoveled a square in the snow on the lake and skated until dark. I had no idea where Nate's self-esteem was that winter, but I admired him for the confidence that remained and his ability to push his problems aside and keep on. I thought he might be an example to look to in my own circumstances. He truly enjoyed himself up there with his kids, chasing them around the rink, tossing them into soft piles of snow. This was the sort of roughhousing our father had done with us and seemed, at those moments, to mean more than anything you could ever say. I was happy to see it and to remember our father like that, fully alive and deeply connected to the people who loved him.

I thought Nate would be fine in the long run—that his competitive nature would win the day if for no better reason than a bloody-minded determination to rub Monica's nose in his happiness. Whatever was happening between Nate and his older son would settle. That's what I decided that first evening up north. He'd fallen out with Titus for a time, but nothing had happened between them that couldn't be corrected, and as the sun slipped behind the trees, I knew things were on the mend now, that at least here my family was coming together and that I was privileged to be part of it.

The afternoon we got back from the cottage, an e-mail from Isabel informed me that she was taking Ava to Paris for Christmas with Pablo, her boyfriend. I stared at the screen and read the message a second time, then stood up and threw the first thing I could find—a coffee mug—against the wall, and it exploded against the Christmas calendar.

"Like *fuck* you are," I said, reaching for the phone.

At that moment, as I heard the call ring through, I hoped Pablo might pick up so I could tell him what a chump asshole he was and how his situation might look rosy right now but just you wait, my friend, your time will come. Sooner or later you'll get a taste of what this backstabbing conniving bitch has in store for you. Oh yes sir, just you wait. And then he'd pass the phone to Isabel, who'd freely admit I'd been right all along and was absolutely in the clear, that the list of mistakes and injustices she'd made in the lead up to this pathetic family drama was as long as her arm and that, yes, Christmas in Paris was the worst idea she'd ever had.

But then she answered the phone.

"You have no right. You hear me?" I said. "No right whatever. Don't think for a second I'm going to let you do this. You know what this is called? This is called child abduction. Kidnapping! She's my daughter, too. We talked about this."

"It's four days. And stop shouting, or I'll hang up."

If I had a second mug to throw, I would've thrown it then. "Four days? You think that's nothing after I haven't seen my daughter in five months? We'll both lose if you want to play that game."

There was a pause. I looked at the Christmas calendar. It was dripping with coffee. The mug was all over the kitchen floor.

"You're forgetting one thing," said the queen of calm, with nothing but killer instinct. "I'm raising our daughter, not you. You left, not me."

She knew the oceans of guilt I was swimming in and was more than willing to hold my head under long enough to remind me that *I'd* gotten on that plane and disappeared, not her.

"You're unbelievable," I said.

"Pablo was never the issue. You know that."

"Put her on the phone," I said.

Half a minute later, when my daughter's voice flooded my heart, I felt the urge to rip open my chest and cry like an eight-year-old girl.

"Hi, Daddy," she said, possibly the two sweetest words in the English language. "Have you heard?"

"You're going to *Paris*."

The futility of my situation had never felt as real to me as it did at that moment. Blindfolded and outnumbered, I was fighting a battle with both hands tied behind my back.

"The Champs-Élysées, the Eiffel Tower, all that stuff you see in pictures! Isn't that wonderful?"

"It sure is. You're a lucky girl. That's a hell of a city."

"And you don't mind, right?"

"Christmas in Paris—who says no to that? Are you kidding?"

"You're not mad at Mom, right?" she said.

"Me? Of course not," I said, switching to Spanish and leaning my forehead against the kitchen cupboard. It had always been a language in which I found it easier to bury my lies.

"Mom's telling me to get off the phone now," she said. "Okay?"

"Okay, sweetheart."

"Okay, Daddy."

She spoke French to me two days later when she called from Pablo's apartment on Boulevard Saint-Michel in Paris. It was as if some brilliant little tour guide was

hanging on the other end of the line extolling the vir-
tues of some new, previously undiscovered kingdom. I
played along, muddling through in my passable French,
prompting her with questions.

"Yes, mademoiselle, and do you like the little mon-
keys in the streets dancing to the accordion music?"

"Oh, yes. And their little hats."

"And the bells they clap together?"

"Those are miniature tambourines, monsieur," she
said.

Her French was beautifully accented, and when
she spoke of Pablo's building, kindly providing the
address, she made it sound like a castle, grand and elegant and five times bigger than the apartment she lived
in back in Madrid. She said she could actually see the
Eiffel Tower from her bedroom window. She'd been to
the Louvre that day and toured through the catacombs
beneath the city. The kicker was the no-holds-barred
shopping spree Pablo had treated them to this morning. I clenched my teeth and told her it sounded like
Christmas in Paris was a dream come true.

After drinking three small whiskeys and a watching a movie I couldn't concentrate on, I Googled a
street view of Pablo's place on the Boulevard Saint-
Michel. Among the sidewalk crowd was a teenage girl
riding a blue bicycle, and for an instant, I thought it
was Ava. According to the date stamp on the images
I trolled through, it was spring, two seasons removed
from the depths of the winter I found myself trapped
in. But when I saw the girl—her lovely cheek and the
small point of an ear under her long, dark hair—my

heart jumped, a powerful surge of hope from points unknown flowed into me, and I stared at who was not but could've been my daughter, lost in thought and willing it to be her as if pondering a marvelous ghost facsimile of my own soul.

I called ahead the next morning and booked a flight, then left a message telling Hilary what was going on. I got Nate on the phone as I rode in the back of the airport limo.

"Hey, brother. What's with you?" he said.

I filled him in on the situation.

"Go get 'em, tiger," he said.

I arrived at check-in buoyed by the thought of my resilience. I was dogged. I'd make it clear that I wouldn't be played or pushed around or back down. It was my right to see my daughter on Christmas Day. After I checked in, I emptied my pockets and passed through the scanner. Because I was traveling with carry-on only, I saw the agent who'd let me through the first layer of security make eye contact with the two manning the scanner. I slipped off my belt, whose buckle was a modest stainless-steel rectangle that might hardly have beeped, and passed without consequence through the X-ray. Nor did I beep when the agent on the other side traced the contours of my arms and legs and chest with his handheld metal detector. But the world had changed, it seemed, and no longer accommodated the father who decided on an impulse to visit his daughter in another country. Nor did it trust men traveling with a single handbag on a ticket purchased that morning. I slipped my belt back on, gathered up the contents of my pockets and moved along, but two agents met me before I hit the escalator and led me back in the direction I'd come from. In a moment I was sitting in a box of a room facing two men who looked just as unhappy to be working on Christmas Eve as I was to be pinned down here, minutes from missing my flight.

"Okay, then. Let's see," the first man said, thumbing through my passport. "Looks like you do a lot of traveling."

The other guy standing to his right obviously took less pleasure in harassing passengers than his partner did.

I told him I owned and operated five international language schools and that travel was an integral part of my business.

"Is that right?" he said.

"Can you tell me what the issue is here?"

He didn't seem interested in answering this question.

"It's Christmas Eve," I said. "I need to get this plane."

"What's in Paris? Is it a problem if I ask you that?"

"My daughter," I said. "No, it's not a problem."

"Family visit, then?"

"Yes."

He continued flipping the pages. "What's your daughter's name?"

"Ava Bellerose," I said.

"She lives in Paris, does she?"

"Just visiting. She lives in Madrid with her mother."

"And these are last-minute travel plans? Spur-of-the-moment sort of thing?"

"Her mother and I don't live together," I said. "I'm adapting to circumstances."

He looked up and smiled. "Good," he said. "I like that. You were in Istanbul last year."

"Yes."

"Why would that be the case?"

"I run five language schools. I told you—three in Spain, one each in Dublin and Toronto. I travel for my business."

"And do you associate with known terrorists, Mr. Bellerose, and are you now or have you ever been involved with any terrorist dealings?"

I couldn't help myself. "Just my ex-wife," I said.

He smiled again. "I see," he said, tilting his head slightly.

"No. Never."

"Nothing beyond your domestic situation, Mr. Bellerose?"

"This is ridiculous. You know it is."

"You understand our concern here."

"I'm answering your questions. I fly twenty times a year and probably have for the past fifteen years. Why all of a sudden do I want to blow up a plane to Paris?"

I was aware that this wasn't helping my case any.

"No one said anything about blowing up planes," he said. He didn't look amused. He never had to begin with, but he looked worse now. He left the room with my passport. The other man stayed with me, his arms crossed over his chest. I watched the hands on the clock on the wall angle closer and closer to the time they'd shut down boarding on my flight. I smiled at my guard and imagined him shuffling me off to some black site where desperate cries from the next cell were the only human communication I'd ever hear again.

The other agent returned with my passport, and he handed it to me and held the door. "Christmas in Paris," he said. "You're one lucky man."

I walked back into the teeming concourse, armpits soaked, knees trembling, and arrived at my gate with two minutes to spare.

It was still dark when I landed at Charles de Gaulle on Christmas morning. I'd slept for an hour or two sometime in the middle of the flight. My heart was racing in my chest, my eyes were burning, and in the distance I saw the red blinking lights of airport support vehicles crisscrossing the tarmac. It looked cold and miserable outside. When I switched on my phone and called Isabel, it rang through to her service. After customs I tried again, then took a taxi to Boulevard Saint-Michel as the morning sun came up through a cloud bank that covered the city. It cast a silver light over the road and against the grey buildings, and as the cab rolled ever closer to my destination, I began to doubt that Ava would be there waiting for me. This hadn't occurred to me before now. What if they'd left for the countryside, maybe even gone back to Madrid? There was no guarantee she'd be anywhere I'd know to look. For a moment the terrifying scenario that I'd never see her again gripped my imagination. Had they kidnapped her for real, I wondered, taken her away to some strange place to start life all over again?

I had the driver wait while I leaned on the intercom with my eyes closed, almost reduced to a state of prayer. I didn't know if I could handle a rejection the size of the one that was shaping up before me. As the tinny buzzing of the intercom ran up through the building's innards, the absurdity of my situation grew obvious in all its grey dimensions. I'd almost turned and started back to the cab when a familiar voice called out.

"Daddy? That's not really you, is it?" she said in Spanish. "Look up. Look up. At the camera!"

The IV drip of Ava's voice flowed into my veins.

"You bet it is, peanut," I said, looking up and giving her a big smile.

"Oh my God. Are you coming up? Come, come. Pablo's smiling at me now."

Of course I had no interest in meeting the man who'd whisked my estranged wife and daughter off to the City of Light. "I'm here to see you, though. I can meet him some other time, all right? Come on down. Tell your mother I'm here and that I want to take you out somewhere. I want to show you off to Paris."

Hands in my pockets, I smiled at the old lady sitting on the red sofa pushed up against the far wall. She held a grey cat in her lap, the snakelike tail the only moving part of this portrait. *"Joyeux Noël,"* I said. She shrugged her narrow shoulders and returned her attention to the cat.

When my daughter appeared a moment later, I picked her up and turned her once in the air the way

I used to when she was little, a greeting we'd perfected over the years. It was a graceful spin involving three steps, my hands gripping at her armpits.

Isabel stood to the side with her arms folded over her chest. She was surprised, first and foremost. She was also furious that I'd discovered their Christmas hideaway in Paris. She was equally impressed, though, it seemed to me at the time, that I'd cared enough to get on a plane and fly through the night to claim some part of this day with my daughter. I was hopped up on adrenaline and caffeine and pleased with myself. The heavy sky outside the lobby window was promising at least a flurry or two, and I had, through this flying visit, trumped any gift or gesture likely to emerge from her mother's new pairing with this celebrated Spaniard.

"We'll talk about this later," she said.

I put my arm around Ava's head in a play headlock. "I'm looking forward to it. Right now this one needs a monster plate of foie. I'm going to fatten up this goose."

Isabel stood at the door of the building and watched us leave. In a moment we got back in the cab and were driving through Paris. I felt like I'd just raided the enemy's storehouse and was escaping with the crown jewels. I asked the driver to take us to Notre-Dame.

"I bet you'd like him," Ava said. "He can talk about lots of things."

"Your mom's new boyfriend, you mean?"

"Pablo. Yes."

"I'm happy to hear that. Mom deserves a nice guy."

"She chose you once upon a time."

"She did, didn't she?"

"He's jealous of you, Daddy."

"I guess that means he and I have a little something in common," I said.

"You're jealous of him?"

"Hey, your mother's a catch, right?" I said. "He's a lucky guy to have her."

Ava turned away and watched the city go by. "I don't think you mean that," she said, still facing the window.

"Why wouldn't I mean that? Of course I do."

"You wouldn't be living in *Canada* if you meant that."

"Of course I would. I've got that new school over there, remember? That takes a lot of my time. *All* my time."

"You think I'm stupid," she said, turning to look at me now. "You think I'm just some stupid kid you can lie to, and I'll just believe whatever you tell me."

The adrenaline high I'd ridden into town on had bottomed out in less time than she needed to finish the thought.

"That's not true," I said.

She made a cutting face, then turned back to the window and watched the beautiful city roll by as she considered the sad reality that had placed us in this cab on a lonely Christmas Day in a foreign place. It all came crashing down on me like the weight of the world because she was right, and now the incomprehensible brainteaser that was our life seemed from this new angle even cloudier than it had just a day before. I reached for my carry-on bag at my feet, zipped it open and pulled out a present.

"I almost forgot," I said. "Merry Christmas."

"Your timing's impeccable," she said, acidly, taking it from me and placing it in her lap without opening it.

"It's a promise from me to you."

"I've had a few of those before," she said.

"Please, open it."

Careful not to demonstrate any enthusiasm, she hooked a finger under the wrapper and tore. "Oh, wow. A book," she said.

"It's a book of promises. Things we'll see and do together when you come over next summer. Go on. Open it to where that bookmark is."

It was the coffee-table book I'd flipped through at Nate's house the day I arrived in Canada six months earlier. She flipped ahead and found the photograph of my brother's cottage.

"There, see?"

"It's a building," she said.

"It's a building, okay. But it's the future, too. It's what you're going to see when you visit me next summer. That's your uncle's cottage. We'll all go up there."

Shot at dusk from the lake, the photograph showed the log cabin, its windows blaring with golden light, framed by a stand of jack pines. In the foreground there was a small white dock with a canoe pulled up alongside.

"Is he rich or something?"

"He must be a little bit, anyway. And you see that tire tied to the tree on the left there?"

"You swing on it, right? I've seen that in movies."

"That'll be you," I said.

The streets of Paris were all but empty this morning. Wreaths were strung from lampposts. A scooter chugged by carrying the driver and his passenger off to some seasonal rendezvous.

"You can swim and read all day there. They have a Jet Ski, too, and a motorboat. But maybe you're more of the canoe type. Let me look at you. Oh, yeah. You're definitely a canoe girl. You won't believe this, but all that water you see in the picture—it was frozen solid when I was there last week."

"You were there last week?"

"It was all white. Snow up to your knees."

"I don't believe that," she said.

"This is Canada we're talking about."

"Did you see any polar bears?"

"No bears. But we could order some."

"Was the ice thick?" she said, smiling now.

"Thick? We skated on it!"

For a kid raised in Madrid I knew this would sound as fantastic as camels in the desert might have seemed to me at that age.

"I guess that's pretty cool," she said.

"You'll love it. That's another promise."

"You're forgetting one thing."

"What's that?"

"Mom would never let me go. I'm just twelve. And *she's* never going to want to go over there."

"No, probably not. But you're thirteen next summer, and that's official teenager status. That's when *you* start telling *us* what to do."

"As if," she said.

"You'll see."

"Anyway, in case you've forgotten, my birthday's at the *end* of the summer."

We got out at the next intersection and walked up into Saint-Germain a few blocks, my carry-on slung over my shoulder. As we waited for a traffic light, Ava slipped her arm in mine, and I pulled her in close to me and kissed the top of her head.

After we got a pastry and some hot chocolate at a little café, we leaned against the balustrade of the Pont Notre-Dame and watched the sightseeing boats passing beneath us.

"You're going to meet someone over there and marry her and have a new family," she said. "And then you're going to just forget about us."

"Is that what you really think?"

She shrugged. "I don't know. It happens all the time."

"Not with me it doesn't. Not in a million years. That boat coming now?" I said, nodding.

"What about it?"

"I'm like that boat," I said.

"Leave it to you to compare yourself to a *boat*."

"Why would you want to sail anywhere else in the world once you've sailed through the heart of Paris? That's what I'm thinking."

➤❙ Eight

I felt reinvigorated after I got back to Toronto, which is to say the guilt and uncertainty that presided over me in those days moved into the background for a time. I knew that a few grey hours in Paris couldn't change the reality that the minutes of my daughter's life were ticking away without me and that with each passing week some pivotal event might occur that could only be narrated to me via Skype. I'd been aware of all this, of course, at least on some level, when her mother and I began discussing the likelihood of my going back to Canada. The end of our marriage, and that stirring notion of freedom that swelled both our heads, had provided the last necessary impetus. The weightlessness that buoyed me lasted only until I realized that I was doing little more than exchanging one set of challenges for another; added to this, I was rarely if ever sure which of the two sets of challenges was more interesting. Freedom's an empty word, I decided. It is, by my measure, the most dangerous word in the English language, at least where it concerns husbands and wives. It is a constant tug, a deceitful promise, a disease that haunts bedrooms and breakfast tables from Whitehorse to Albuquerque. When I'd made the decision to leave, I believed—astonishingly, it seems to me now—that it was in my grasp.

When I saw Hilary a few days after getting back, she hauled out my belated Christmas present. She'd noticed the notepads I left around the house, pulled them together and wrapped them in a Christmas bow. I looked through them that afternoon, as if for the first time. Some of them weren't bad, I thought. The character I'd been trying to get right since I was a kid was a stripped down Waldo rip-off who spent most of his time skateboarding past or into unusual situations— bank robberies, space invasions, earthquakes. As part of the package she'd included the receipt for a ten-week comics-drawing class at a downtown community college. (The amount she'd paid was blacked out, with a happy face drawn beside it.) She told me she wasn't going to take it personally if I didn't like the class and had to drop it. I'd seemed stressed lately, she said, and she figured something like this might help me relax.

The academy had its grand opening the second week in January. I'd flown in a handful of agents and reps and put on a small presentation and a big banquet that ended up lasting well into the night. The majority of the students who'd enrolled were from Spain and Japan, a few from Mexico and South Korea. We were at something like 28 percent capacity, but it was early days yet. That first winter term would serve as a test-drive that would ease us into the high summer season when bookings were already looking strong.

I was putting in five long days a week now working

out the kinks and training staff. I had the European schools to look after, too. Come Saturday morning I'd wake up to find Hilary sleeping beside me and feel that wonderful new body against mine and think for a minute that maybe I could do this, that perhaps there was a future for me here after all. Possibly I'd broken the back of that slump that had held me for too long, and I was just steps away from turning that fiction of a marvelous bachelorhood year into a reality.

Saturday mornings were a good time for us. There was never any place we needed to be before noon, so we lounged around half naked and drowsy, in no special hurry to wake up, and eventually prepared an indulgent breakfast, had sex in surprising corners of the house, scrubbed each other's back in the shower and read the business sections of the papers over a third cup of coffee. Hilary led a spinning class at a gym on the lakeshore on Saturday afternoons. After she left, I'd check messages to see if anything was going on over in Spain, and if there wasn't I'd walk down to Nate's house to see what was up.

If Titus and Quinn had a weekend with their mother, I'd cycle over to the downtown YMCA, just a few blocks up from the academy, and pound the heavy bag on the third floor until the tingling in my jaw and the back of my head started up. I'd picked up some gloves after tearing up my knuckles a few months earlier, but I wasn't much of a boxer. Still, dancing around that bag got my heart pumping better than anything I'd ever done. Sometimes guys who really knew what they were doing showed up and started working out. They'd wear plastic bags over their hoodies to help them get used to the extreme temperatures they'd feel in the ring, and they'd move their hands and feet with a beauty and rhythm I could've watched for hours. One of them, Milton, was a small sinewy guy in his late twenties with skin as black as the man's I'd sold that stolen picture frame to years earlier in Spain. He was leaning against the wall watching me while he taped his hands.

"How long you been doing this?" he said.

I told him.

"Okay, man. Watch this."

So I stepped aside, and he showed me, point by point, what I was doing wrong.

"Okay. Look, when you do this . . . no, no, not like that, man. Why aren't you listening? Come on, brother. Do it again."

Between rounds on the heavy bag I'd lean on the railing overlooking the basketball courts in the gym on the first floor. There were always kids down there shooting hoops or doing Tae Kwon Do. Sweating and breathing like I'd just come off a 10K run, I'd watch what was happening for a minute or two, then start up again for as long as I could stand it. I'd pound away for ten or fifteen minutes until my lungs started burning and I felt that electricity coursing through my body—a strange, prickling sensation that was entirely new to me—until I had to crouch against the wall gulping for air and consciously tell myself that this wasn't the day

I was going to fall over and die in front of a bunch of strangers. When I finally got my heart rate back down to normal, I'd change for the pool and swim until I barely had the strength to haul myself up out of the water.

My first drawing class fell on a Wednesday evening near the end of January, not long after the academy's official opening. I stayed at work late that day, hiked up my collar and walked the ten blocks through a heavy snowfall over to the School of Design on Adelaide Street. I was tired, an unremarkable state for me at that point, and casting around in my memory for happy thoughts about my daughter. I think I'd just put my Japanese contact back on a plane after a night on the town. I was feeling drained and woozy, and all I wanted to do was go home and fall into bed. I'd give it try, though, just to say I'd given it a fair shake; then I'd drop the class and buy Hilary a couple dozen roses and take her out for dinner to let her know the gesture had been appreciated.

I entered through the student gallery and found studio 2. There were seven of us in the class, the most talented a tall, slim Croatian named Suada whom I pegged to be in her midthirties. She wore all black and composed incredible panels that showed snipers hiding in church towers or hotel rooms as little kids and mothers picked through the streets for firewood. As far as I could tell no one else had nearly as much to say about the world as she did. I don't think I heard her speak two words the whole ten weeks. I noticed her that first day looking at the art taped to the exposed brick studio wall before the instructor walked in and started assigning easels.

At first I thought Vincent was another student. He was a pointy-bearded man with slender fingers, somewhere in his late fifties, I guessed, and introduced himself that evening with a round of handshakes and said he was looking forward to working with us. By the end of that first class I decided to stick with it.

He liked to start by bringing out a series of favorite frames or comic strips and explaining what made them special. He said there was a perfect work of art inside all of us but that only someone gifted and disciplined was able to bring it out into the light of day. After one of these introductions we'd settle in and work on some drawing exercises while he walked around the studio and asked, leaning over a shoulder, exactly what you were trying to get at. Most of us knew enough about drawing to realize that only the Croatian really had anything to offer. Once he used Suada's work as an example of a great use of perspective; she had a frame of a sniper's bullet spinning toward the viewer that I just couldn't take my eyes off. He never talked about story arcs or blocking figures. That was comic-book territory, "and way beyond most of you," but he liked to ask questions like "What's this guy supposed to be doing?" or "Is there a reason this head's so small?" I imagined he was one of those community-college teachers who'd been saved from economic ruin by a steady job and was toiling late into the night in a brightly lit basement studio on some epic comics masterpiece. But he never brought in his own work, not being the sort, he told us, to talk about a work in progress.

Four or five weeks in, sometime in early March, I saw him coming up from the lockers, his red scarf already wrapped around his neck, a black wool cap set on his head, ears uncovered. He had a backpack in his right hand.

"That was a good class," I said as we walked down a colorless hallway.

"Some talented artists in the group."

"But no Stan Lees, I guess," I said, putting my bike helmet on and fastening the snap under my chin. I'd bought it after seeing a courier get doored a few weeks earlier. The guy at the bike shop told me cyclists in the city were dropping like flies, getting their heads squashed, femurs crushed, arms busted.

"Cold night to ride," Vincent said.

"I'm not that far, anyway."

"Stick with it," he said. "Exercise is a good habit. Artists rarely have those." He opened the glass door that looked out onto Adelaide Street. "Can you ride with a beer or two in you?"

"I don't see why not," I said. Hilary was staying over that night, but she had an early morning appointment. I called her to say I was grabbing a beer with my instructor, and ten minutes later I was sitting at the bar facing an aquarium full of marvelously colored tropical fish and listening to Vincent talk.

He mentioned artists and genres and styles I'd

never heard of. I didn't have any opinions regarding these things but tried to keep up and probably was pleased that he took me seriously enough to want to talk to me. Conversation eventually moved on to general matters. Back in the nineties he'd lived in San Francisco and worked in advertising. I gave him the thumbnail sketch of my life in Spain, my failed marriage, my beautiful daughter, the language academies. I handed him one of my business cards, which he examined with minimal interest.

"Nice and clean," he said, then gave it back to me.

He'd been involved in some high-flying campaigns over the years. None of them rang a bell, I admitted, but that was likely due to the fact that I'd been away for so long. He'd turn sixty-one in May, he said, and had hated every minute of his sixteen years in advertising. Following a cancer scare that came and went about ten years ago now, he'd gotten up the courage to quit. His marriage fell apart not long after that.

"We get along better now than we ever did," he said. "That's the secret. Get out while you can. Before the silence turns toxic."

Apparently he hadn't looked back, this man. There didn't seem to be a nostalgic bone in his body, no regrets, no living in the past. Things were good. He wouldn't mind having the sort of money he used to make, he said, and he missed his son, who was backpacking through Thailand as we spoke, but that had nothing to do with changing jobs or leaving his marriage.

"What about teaching?" I said. "You like it?"

"Sure, I do. I like that I can tell people what I know and think without them getting pissed off at me. That's essentially untrue in any other walk of life. People usually don't want advice unless they're paying for it."

"I'd say you're right about that," I said.

I could only guess that teaching at a community college didn't satisfy him aesthetically, since Vincent—based on the secrecy he shrouded his work in—considered himself an artist. But he was cheerful during class and listened intently when one of us explained to him over smudged graphite what it was we were trying to achieve. (The truth was we weren't really trying to achieve all that much, other than clearing our heads after another uneventful Wednesday.) He seemed cheerful tonight, too, and when I reached for my wallet, he touched my hand and waved over the bartender, a heavyset redhead. "This guy thinks you're going to take his money," he told her.

She said, "He don't know our Vincent very well then, does he?"

I could have sat there all night. She had a friendly bartender vibe about her and made it look like she enjoyed nothing more than pushing pints over that shiny mahogany bar top. A loop of eighties power pop rolled out at half volume from the speakers clamped to the brick wall behind us.

"Well, let's make it even then," I said. "What do you say to two more?"

"I wouldn't argue," Vincent said.

She replaced our glasses with fresh ones.

"Thank you," I said.

"Not a problem," she said, then moved off to serve a bent-back old guy down at the far end of the bar. A yellow fish the size of my little finger nibbled up and down the aquarium wall and around the silhouette of a black catfish that had pasted itself to the glass.

"No regrets, then?" I said.

"You lost me," he said.

"I mean about your ex."

"Water under the bridge of a circular river," he said with a grin, tracing his finger around the circumference of his pint glass.

"You want to hear a story?" I said.

"That's what they invented pubs for."

So I told him about Christmas in Paris and that, while I'd come back feeling okay about things, I was now so full of yearning and guilt that I thought my heart was going to explode. When I'd dropped Ava off at Pablo's that afternoon, I told Isabel about the promise I'd made to Ava about bringing her over next summer. This was bad timing, and it didn't go over well, and now I wondered if I hadn't blown it entirely.

"Kidnapping, eh?"

"That's what it felt like. It just kind of reminded me how little say I have in all this."

He nodded, thinking about his own life, maybe, or that he'd opened a can of worms he'd rather close down tight again. His face was hard to read. "No two ways about it," he said.

"I'm listening."

"You need to get her over here," he said. "You've got

to get your daughter involved in this new life you're setting up for yourself. It's basic math, genius. You're in a holding pattern. Life here is nothing but a long, sad, shitty holiday away from home until your daughter comes over and proves it isn't."

"I don't know if that's ever going to happen," I said.

"Why not?"

"Her mother shut that down. When I brought it up in Paris, she looked at me like I had two heads."

Confusion clouded over Vincent's face as if he suddenly were hearing a different conversation. "I'm sorry, I don't quite follow. Because she looks at you funny you're giving up? Did I hear that right?"

"It's not as easy as it sounds," I said.

"You flew over there unannounced and showed her you've got some balls left. Okay. So far so good. What's your next step?"

"I'm not sure I have one."

"You've got a lot left in your stride, trust me. Your job isn't to accommodate this aberration, my friend. That's done with. You've got to take hold of this bough and shake it until fruit starts falling from the tree. You hear me? You've got to put your fucking foot down."

"So says the expert?"

"You better believe it," he said.

We ended our night together by shaking hands outside on the sidewalk. It was snowing now, and the sky was black, and dark buildings loomed overhead. Vincent pulled his wool hat down over his ears and said, "Good night, Charlie. Slippery roads. You watch yourself."

The roads, slippery as they might have been, were pretty much mine that night after I cleared the downtown core. I burned a few red lights and hopped a few curbs along Gerrard and was coming up to Parliament at a good clip when my front tire caught in a streetcar track and I went headfirst over the handlebars. I must've blacked out for a second. When I came to, I was flat on my back and watching the snow fall through the cone of yellow light from the streetlamp on the corner. Just inches from my head, my front tire spun resolutely; I thought I'd broken my right shoulder. Every time I tried to budge, a razor of pain shot through it. I pulled myself off the road and over to the curb. It took a few attempts to sit up, but I finally managed to, and that's when my shoulder popped back into its socket.

Hilary was out cold when I arrived home. I got undressed and checked for bruises, then swallowed three or four Tylenols and crawled into bed. With two pints and those pills in me, I thought I had a good chance of getting a half-decent sleep. What I hadn't figured on was anyone calling me in the middle of the night.

It was around two o'clock when the phone rang. Nate sometimes liked to call from the road, not to check in—his boys were with their mother that night—but to let me know how much fun he was having or, conversely, to bitch and moan about some new "cuntism" Monica had just pulled. I was used to listening patiently while he got whatever he needed to get off his chest—mostly something about that Swedish boyfriend of Monica's, whom he suspected was moving in on fatherly duties with the boys. He had no evidence of this, of course, at least to my knowledge. They'd never even met, I knew, but he had theories and opinions that I supposed were based on little more than what his sons let slip and his own sense of the ever-increasing injustice.

More and more often now he talked about how unfair everything was for a father these days—the courts, custody, all that. He often had been drinking, certainly enough to drop his tendency to come off as flashy and polished and likable. But after blowing off some steam, his mood might lift, and we'd end on a positive note, some story about racking up an exorbitant bar tab with clients and now kicking back at the marina with his feet up, basking in the moonlight over the Gulf—and wasn't life grand for those savvy enough to figure it out? He was usually half in the bag, but I'd steer him in a direction that I hoped might bring him back into the steadiness you need when you're alone on the road, and then we'd finally sign off. Usually, when he called in the next day or two, he'd have no recollection of the earlier conversation, and it was as if I'd dreamed it all up.

And then in my mind's eye I imagined Ava sitting at the breakfast table back home in Madrid, crying and in desperate need to talk to me. That was another possibility. Or was it Isabel calling to say that our daughter was hurt? All this flashed through my mind between rings, and now, forgetting about my shoulder, I rolled over and felt that same agonizing pop all over again.

"Who was that?" Nate said, when I took the phone

from Hilary. She'd answered it while I was putting my shoulder back in place.

"Who else could it be?" I said. "It's Hilary. You know what time it is?"

In the silence on the other end of the line I could hear him thinking, maybe looking out over a seascape bathed in warm moonlight and smoking one of those great cigars.

"What's up?" I said. "You okay?"

"Yeah. I'm good."

"Okay," I said. "Can I go back to sleep?"

"That's Hilary with you?"

"What do you mean?"

"It sounded like Monica, you know, when she answered. I know my wife's voice."

"And I know what you sound like when you're drunk."

"You're fucking my wife, aren't you?"

"I'm hanging up now," I said.

In the cold light of morning I wondered if he'd remember the phone call. I didn't believe he actually meant what he'd said. He knew Hilary was staying at my place two or three nights a week in those days and that any woman answering my phone in the middle of the night would have to be her. I decided he'd been either drunk or determined to put me on my back foot, though I had no idea why he'd want to do that. That was the sort of game he'd played when he stayed with us in Madrid all those years ago, a strange and pointless badgering that seemed an end in itself as far as I could tell.

He usually seemed fine when he got home after a trip. He'd step out from the airport limo hale and smiling, the picture of his old sporting self, and as if to prove something to me, or to himself, he'd convene a game of catch or touch football or soccer, followed by a couple beers on the back deck, at which point he'd tell me how much fun he was having as a bachelor, how this should have happened years ago.

I decided that what he craved was his youth. He wanted sunshine and blue water and the thrill of sport to return him to the quickened spirits he'd had before getting married. He didn't speak about the old days very much, but his hobbies and recreations were those of a man who would never be dislodged from better days long gone.

He often brought a gift for the boys and a bottle of wine or cognac for me. In exchange Quinn would give him a heavy high five or fist bump, then run off with his new autographed football or baseball glove to add to his collection. But Titus, who over a weekend with me and his brother might have shown indications that he wasn't as pissed off at his mom and dad as I knew he was, and who lately had smiled through the Mel Brooks films we watched and actually said something positive from time to time, would roll his shoulders and sneer and offer some sarcastic comment that Nate couldn't just ignore. "That's a nice way to greet your old man," he might say, masking his anger or disappointment with locker-room irony. "See how this peckerhead talks to his dad?"

He didn't look or act any different when he came by the house later that day after he got back from Florida. He seemed in high spirits and was full of stories about his fresh triumphs. My shoulder still wasn't feeling very good, and when we shook hands I must've flinched. "Something wrong there, champ?" he said. I almost expected him to refer to the phone call then, maybe to laugh it off and tell me I was a serious dick who couldn't take a joke. But he didn't. Instead he asked if I wanted to take a spin up to "the Swede's" house. That's how he always referred to Monica's boyfriend. I supposed denying the man a real name made it all just a bit easier for Nate. But he needed to pick up his kids in a few minutes, so did I want to tag along?

It was a ten-minute drive from door to door, barely long enough for two songs to come and go on the car stereo but more than enough time for my brother's mood to visibly shift into a silent, gnawing anxiety.

There was nothing in my brother's rival's Rosedale neighborhood for less than two million dollars. It was clear that Kaj Adolfsson was a bigger success than he could ever be. In business and in love he'd beaten him hands down, no contest, and as Nate pulled the Escalade up to the curb, and I asked him if he was okay, he looked at me, winked and said, "Peachy, couldn't be fucking better," then leaned on the horn.

I should have seen that coming. He wasn't about to knock. Instead, he got out of the car, crossed his arms over his chest and watched the palatial house with a sneering eye. It was a big grey monster and artfully landscaped, with a low fieldstone wall rising up from the lawn and running parallel to the sidewalk.

I got out, too, and stood beside my brother in the cold. There was snow on the ground, and the sky was brooding with heavy blue clouds. It was midafternoon. Nate reached into the car and honked again, and finally the front door opened and Quinn appeared and waved, went quickly back inside and emerged a moment later carrying a backpack and wearing a wool hat and a blue ski jacket. Nate scooped up a snowball and threw it, and Quinn lunged and caught it and tossed it back at us. He was in the car and thumbing away at his GameBoy before Titus appeared a minute later. Waiting there on the other side of the stone wall, I saw the hesitation and regret in his face when he turned to his mother, as if reiterating the case he'd been making all week, or all month, that he didn't want to leave. She was standing in the doorway with him, and I knew Nate saw it, too, and I felt more for him at that moment than I ever had in my life. He knew the battle was lost. The boy couldn't have put a finer point on it, and when he kissed his mom and then shook hands with the man who suddenly appeared beside them, I swear I almost heard my brother's heart die.

For that trip Nate gave me a fifteen-year-old single malt. Quinn got *Call of Duty 3*. And for Titus, a baseball bat autographed by some renowned slugger. He brought out these presents after we got back to their place. Titus tapped the bat against the kitchen tile, rolled his eyes, then said in a weirdly squeaky Sponge-Bob voice, "Good for bashing heads."

Nate called Monica a few hours later, when the kids were upstairs watching TV. I could feel my own heart pounding with anxiety as they spoke.

"You think so?" he said. "You think it's fucking normal that a kid should say something about bashing heads? No. Not even remotely possible. And then I hear this—"

After abruptly hanging up he swore and started pacing the room.

"It'll pass," I said. "I know it's tough."

"Yeah. Maybe when those kids grow up and realize what a bitch their mother was. But I've got to live with this. I'll have to put up with this for the next twenty years."

He was rattled, as I would've been, but I thought he'd try to turn the point to his advantage, refer to it as justification for the comment he'd made about her sleeping with me—that it was making him crazy. He didn't, though. He just kept steaming away, lost in the outrage of seeing his son shake hands with the devil.

A week later I went by to see how they were holding up. Nate was in the basement, packing a cardboard box to overflowing with items and keepsakes from when we were kids.

"Artifacts from the twilight zone," he said. "Maybe

you want some of this stuff. It's been down here for years."

I was surprised our uncle hadn't thrown everything out when he sold the house and moved away and that he'd had the foresight to pass it along to Nate. I went through the box, my amazement and wonder growing with each new discovery. An old sketchbook of mine fattened with drawings. A stringless yo-yo, a glass jar of beach stones and seashells, a scented green rabbit's foot, a compass, a Staedtler Mars geometry set, a broken whistle and a cracked magnifying glass. All this was like a great puzzle I was hardly able to make heads or tails of. There was a leather pouch filled with Greek coins, a Signet edition of *Hamlet,* a baseball cap fitted for a ten-year-old head and a glass paperweight with a red-and-green angler's fly in its centre. On the bottom of the box was a copy of *Rubber Soul,* with familiar initials inscribed on the back. I hadn't seen it in years. Miles had lent me this record before he left for Montreal that first time, when I was still in high school and dreaming about following him off to university on the greatest adventure of our lives.

Nate asked if I wouldn't mind looking after the kids that night—he had a hot date—and I said I'd be happy to. After he left we got a couple movies and a pizza and had a boys' night.

I was glad to hear about the possibility of a new woman in my brother's life. I knew what seeing Hilary had done for me; if not a cure for a broken heart, it was at least a fine distraction while you tended to the tough stuff in your life. Isabel and I weren't at each other's throats like Nate and Monica were, far from it, but I understood that the situation between us might shift and darken, that in the life of a troubled family there was always room for tragedy.

After the first movie we raided the fridge and made baloney-and-mustard sandwiches. While we were eating, Titus asked if I wanted to see him cry milk. Taken by complete surprise, I asked him what that meant.

"Cry milk," he said. "Seriously. It's exactly what it sounds like."

"I'd pay to see that." I laid out five dollars on the kitchen island.

He raised the glass to his nose and drew a small quantity of milk up into his sinuses, lowered the glass and plugged his nose with his fingers, then leaned forward as he bore down, and magically a white bead grew in the corner of his left eye and rolled down his cheek. He burst out laughing and pocketed the money. I was astonished, at once grossed out and impressed. With a talent like that, I told him, the world was at his feet. "This could get on TV," I said.

Well before seeing him shake hands with Kaj Adolfsson, I'd noticed that Titus was a lot happier when his old man wasn't around. I wanted to chalk it up to some evolutionary struggle between a father and his firstborn son but frankly didn't know what was going on between them. I always dropped indirect praise in his father's direction when Nate was away and pointed out that the reason he worked so hard was because of them; he was concerned for their future, worried about them all the time and couldn't wait to get home to be with them. In effect, everything I was hoping someone was telling Ava about my absence from her life. Sometimes I even believed what I was saying. Titus would just keep doing whatever he was up to when I said these things, staring at the TV or looking down at the food on his plate, and he never challenged my assertions. Sometimes he'd shrug, but generally he let what I said slip away, whether unnoticed or internally mocked, I couldn't be sure. Quinn didn't seem to need my help. I knew he looked up to his father. My brother wasn't around all that much, but when he was they played street hockey or basketball out front, and that seemed to be all this boy needed. It was a physical, easy sort of engagement that Nate was good at. Quinn occasionally wondered out loud why his mom and dad couldn't live together anymore or why they didn't just buy a bigger house so their bedrooms would be farther apart. At which Titus would say there wasn't a house big enough for that anywhere. Quinn never really talked about his mother's boyfriend other than to say that he liked going to Wonderworld. But the moment Titus made milk stream from his eye, it was clear to me that something in him remained essentially pure and innocent, and if he hated his dad, at least that hatred hadn't spiraled out of control into the wider world. He wasn't so far cowed by his father's indifference that he couldn't have fun and enjoy stupid little moments like this. What I needed from him, and what he anted up that evening, was an essential statement of his boyhood. He was still a kid.

Titus showed me the secret when I told him this was a trick I couldn't live without. His brother and I listened to his instructions, and then we both tried it. I couldn't stand the feeling of milk crawling up my nose like a cold finger. The moment I felt it approaching the spot behind my eyeball, I blew a heavy stream from my nose over the table, and they both burst out laughing and laughed until they practically rolled off their seats.

What was certain was that fifteen years from now they'd spill their guts to a wife or girlfriend or therapist about how disastrously their parents had destroyed each other's prospects of happiness, as well as the push and pull of hating and loving them and wishing them dead or remarried or in love all over again in the same lightning, contradictory thought.

I knew that Quinn and Titus needed to be with their mother. Their dad was a distant second best, and I began to suspect that what he was going through was bigger than the end of a marriage, though I really had no idea. I wondered if he was hiding a bankruptcy or some crushing lawsuit. And I was prepared to listen if he wanted to start talking. But I knew Monica's new boyfriend was like a pitchfork in his guts, as Pablo was in mine. His only solution to this was to despise her and start sleeping with every woman in sight, which is what I thought he was doing on all those trips of his. Maybe in the short run he needed to bury himself in some temporary fantasy. Eventually the vitriol against Monica would fade, and he'd settle into a quietly resentful and outwardly smooth bachelorhood.

He didn't come home that night. I hoped that my heartsick and chronically selfish brother, despite the odds and all the patterns he'd traced through his life, had met a nice girl. I don't tend toward fairy tales but was almost optimistic that night after I got his kids to bed. I thought maybe he'd found a woman who might teach him, by her own steady measure of strength and generosity, that there was power and comfort in beneficence and that he still had something positive to give.

Then, just before two o'clock, a knock on his front door woke me up. Thinking Nate had locked himself out, I wrapped myself in his housecoat, went downstairs and opened the door. It wasn't Nate.

"You Nathaniel?" the man said. He was overweight, about fifty and wore a nice suit with a red carnation in his lapel. It looked like he was coming from a fancy event.

I told him it was a bit late to be knocking on the doors of people you didn't even know to look at.

He muttered a quick apology, then turned and walked to the big white SUV idling on the curb, climbed in and pulled away. After watching the taillights disappear, I went upstairs and started snooping through Nate's desk, dresser drawers and bedroom closets. I had no idea what I was looking for. The two possibilities that had crossed my mind were equally troubling. First, that this guy was the boyfriend or husband of the woman Nate had taken out that night. Or that I was looking for pills or a Baggie that might have been intended for this late-night visitor.

"Someone driving a white SUV Benz came by last night," I said the next morning. Nate was texting at the kitchen island, a mug of coffee steaming beside him. "Any idea what he was looking for? He thought I was you."

"Tall thin guy?"

"On the fat side actually."

He shrugged. "No clue."

I walked home with Miles's copy of *Rubber Soul* tucked under my arm. I left it on the kitchen counter while I made some business calls and tried to organize the day in my head. But my thoughts kept turning to Holly. The obsession I'd felt after seeing her for the first time in years had softened by then. But it was still there, buried like a seed, and that old Beatles record, like a spot of sunshine, brought it curling back up to the surface.

⇥| Nine

In the early spring we learned that Titus was playing hooky. He'd been doing this for close to two weeks when Monica called me at work to say that the police had picked him up on Yonge Street, just a few blocks south of the academy. She wanted me to come over and try to talk some sense into him. Nate was traveling—"not that he'd have any idea how to talk to his son"—and wouldn't be home until the weekend. So I drove over and knocked on their door.

Kaj Adolfsson opened it with a smile on his face. "Come on in," he said. When I stepped forward, he shut the door behind me and offered to take my coat.

"I won't be staying long," I said.

"Okay, you'll be wanting to speak with Monica?" he said in that strange singsong accent of his.

He was a handsome man with sharp blue eyes, a few inches shorter than me, and balding. He wore a greying blond Frank Zappa–style mustache and goatee that drew your attention away from that shiny pate of his.

I'd been feeling like a traitor since the minute I agreed to do Monica this favor, and now it only got worse. Stepping through that threshold had compro-

mised whatever loyalty my brother might have reason-
ably expected of me. Here was a summit in progress,
agreed to by me and held in enemy territory. Only a
few hours earlier I'd spoken with Nate as he'd passed
through some airport in the Midwest, caught between
planes. Of course I'd failed to mention my plans for
the evening, that I'd be standing in the Swede's living
room making nice. I wondered now if this had been
a strategic misstep. My brother would hear about it,
surely, and the fact that I'd set foot in the house of the
man who had stolen his wife would erase any purchase
I'd gained with him since coming back. He'd see it as
nothing but the betrayal I myself might have felt if
he'd agreed to a secret meeting with Pablo on the far
side of the Atlantic.

The foyer, whose centrepiece was a spiral staircase
leading to the second floor, was the size of an average
living room. I stood silently, waiting, as he went to the
stairs and called up.

"Nathaniel's brother is here."

I felt something turn inside me that I can only
describe as nostalgia and regret when I heard Monica's
response echo around up there. What I heard was the
voice of a woman who already seemed at home in her
new life. It wasn't the nature of Monica's sudden shift
that astounded me—that she could end up so quickly
in another man's bed—but the envy that weighed on
my heart. Here stood the victor, the balding Frank
Zappa look-alike, the Swedish version of my constitutional court lawyer, the man whose heart and entrails
my brother ate every night in his dreams.

Going Home Again

Nate, who at that very moment might have been standing at some airport hotel window staring soulfully over a bleak America, was defeated. Whom did he have left but me, his only brother and last ally? By his reckoning his wife had begun cheating on him sometime shortly after Titus's tenth birthday. He should've known what was happening, he said, but hadn't picked up on the signs. Suddenly, out of the blue, his terminally grumpy wife was all smiles, which was, to a slightly lesser degree, what had happened in my own case. Isabel, busier than ever and dutifully occupied with committees and meetings and late dinners with friends I barely knew and associates I'd never heard of, seemed to breeze in and out of our home like a harried movie star dropping in for a quick wardrobe change. She played the role well enough for Ava to believe that her mother was entering into a demanding and exciting new phase in her life. My brother had no idea what Monica was up to until the day he got home after a trip and saw that half her closets had been cleared out. He said he sat down on the edge of their bed and cried, though I have a hard time believing this. In my own story Isabel had inched her wedding band off her finger and slid it quietly across the breakfast table and said she had something to tell me.

I found Titus and his mother sitting at a computer in his bedroom on the second floor watching YouTube videos of Japanese kids on skateboards smacking themselves against sidewalks and lampposts. They waved me in, and I watched a couple of spectacular wipeouts with them, and then Monica, who was dressed in jeans and a light blue sweatshirt, led me out of the room and downstairs.

"Titus doesn't want to go back to his father's house," she said. "He hates it there." There was a serving window between the kitchen and the living room, where Monica and I sat facing each other. Hearing the fridge door open and plates clattering, I knew Kaj was hovering back there somewhere.

"I was hoping you'd help prepare Nate for this," she said.

"You want *me* to tell him? I don't think that's my place."

"Just start easing him into the thought. I don't know. He can't even look at me anymore without calling me some name."

She seemed nervous, almost afraid. I guessed it wasn't an easy thing for her to ask me.

"I'm thinking of the boys," she said. "It's mostly you who takes care of them, anyway. I know that."

"Maybe Titus just needs time. It's still pretty fresh, right?"

"You know what your brother's like. He's not changing."

Kaj entered the living room now and handed me a glass of beer. His uncomfortable expression—he was trying to smile—told me he knew exactly why I'd been called here.

"My brother may have trouble showing it," I said, "but he loves those kids. He's just—"

"Loving your kids doesn't make you a good father," she said.

This was true. You could love your child up and down with every last fiber in your heart and soul and still be a shitty parent. You can fuck them up every which way and have no idea that you're doing it. I wondered how much of that statement had been directed at me. She knew the basics of my story, of course, but beyond that she'd have her own theories and speculations. Did she think I was as cold and irresponsible as my brother was? I didn't think so. I reasoned that she might not appreciate that I'd gradually been taking over his fatherly duties. Did she believe Isabel had asked me to clear out of my daughter's life, like she wanted Nate out of their sons'? It was an uncomfortable parallel that hadn't occurred to me before now. Maybe she thought I knew something about dilemmas like the one we were facing now. Did she think I'd been on the receiving end of such a conversation and now might apply some much-needed experience to my brother's case?

"Does Quinn feel the same?" I said.

"No."

I took a sip of beer and leaned back in my seat and thought things through. "Let me talk to him," I said.

"Good."

"I mean Titus."

Upstairs I found him reading on his back on the floor in his bedroom, the book positioned in his two hands like a small shield between his face and the ceiling light. He seemed relaxed and gripped by what he was reading, the most recent novel by Holly's author, the young man we'd seen at the fair in September.

"*Hola,*" Titus said.

"There's hope for you yet."

"*Yo quiero* Taco Bell."

"I'm impressed," I said.

"Isn't it *awe*some?" He grimaced, let out a loud fart, then went back to his reading. I waited for him to stop giggling.

"Listen, Titus," I said. "Your mom says you'd rather stay here. I get that."

"Oh, yeah?"

"You're not getting along with your dad."

He shrugged.

"I guess he's not in town much these days," I said.

"I hadn't noticed."

"Is that the only reason?"

"I like it here," he said, shrugging again. He turned the book over on his chest. "It's awesome. This place is a mansion. There's practically a TV in every room."

"I wonder if you should think a bit more about this before we talk to your dad. Can you do that?"

"Are you two really related?" he said.

"We're not that different." I'd meant to suggest that my brother had some reserve of good sense that would surprise his son one day, though when I said these words it sounded more like a nod toward some waiting calamity, that both my brother and I were turned in the wrong direction. "Your dad's busy. I think that's all it is." The lie almost caught in my throat.

"You actually give a shit about other people, not just yourself," he said. "Or is that a big lie, too?"

"It's just easier for an uncle. And I'm not such a great dad, either. Look at me. I'm over here, and my daughter's back in Spain." I reached down and lifted the book off his chest and read the first line on the open page.

"It's nowhere near as good as his last one," he said, taking it back.

"Your dad's a complicated guy. Maybe that runs in the family. But he loves you guys."

"You're divorced, too, right?"

"Soon to be."

"Are you sad about that?"

"Yes."

"And what about your daughter? Is she sad about it?"

"Yes."

"Why don't you and her mom just make up?" he said.

It was a question I couldn't answer. "I don't know," I said. "People change. Time changes people." It was one of those stupid adult evasions he'd heard a hundred times in his life, I was sure. I regretted pulling him out of the forgetfulness of his book.

"Okay. Tell me this: if getting a divorce is so great," he said, "then why's everybody still so miserable? Why are you miserable? Why's my mom always so sad?"

"Everything always works out in the end. You'll see."

"Mr. Everything's Fine."

"Just think about it a bit more, okay? Your dad's back in a few days. We'll figure something out. In the meantime, stop ditching school."

The look on his face told me he wasn't convinced. The screen saver on the laptop we'd been watching skateboarding videos on showed a number of sharks swimming back and forth in front of a sunken pirate ship. He was watching the screen now, maybe lost in thought. I touched the top of his head. "Let me know how you like that book, okay?"

I found my host standing beside the coffee table downstairs holding a weird-looking rifle and vest. "You okay?" he said.

"I'm good."

"You've got to give this a try."

"What is it?"

"You'll love it," he said. "It's the latest model in the laser-tag market. Just got it in up at the place. The kids are eating it up."

I'd heard all about Wonderworld by then. They had Whirlyball, paintball, sports courts and indoor mini-golf, arcade and redemption games, simulators and batting cages. Their laser-tag facilities were the jewel in the crown. Kids from all around donned futuristic vests and goggles and set out in pursuit of one another in one of four different landscapes—jungle, war zone, planet ZOINKS and the Old West.

"Hand that vest over," I said.

I slipped it on and held my hands up in the air.

He shot me three times at point-blank range. "How do you like that?" he said. "Zing, zing, zing."

It felt like a finger jabbing my heart.

I took Titus and Quinn to a movie later that week. Their dad was out of town again, Cincinnati, then Dunedin, then Naples. I'd said nothing to him about my conversation with Monica, though I'd left the question open in my own mind. Like I said, it wasn't my place, and I was also afraid that sharing this with him might set him off on some path I wasn't prepared to follow. I imagined again the sense of betrayal he'd feel. It would be a final crushing of the spirit. I then wondered if my leaving Madrid had something to do with avoiding putting Ava in the position where she'd have to choose between me and her mother, knowing that I'd barely have a fighting chance if it actually came down to that. I worried, too, how news of Titus's dissatisfaction would make their relationship even more adversarial than it already was.

At the movie I sat in the aisle seat next to Quinn. Up on the screen a man's brains exploded from his head, and the villain holding the weapon grimaced and wiped the blood from his cheek. Halfway through the film, Quinn whispered that he had to use the washroom. I stood waiting outside the men's room and watched the teenagers we'd bought our popcorn and Cokes from at the concession stand. With buds plugged into their ears, their heads bobbing in unison, they were having a great time. The girl wore a railroad track of braces in her mouth. She smiled, much like Ava did, first broadly and unconsciously, then quickly drew her upper lip down over the teeth. The sound of machine guns crackled up from the theatre. What bank robbery was I missing, I wondered. What soppy kiss, when the silence returned, had I been spared?

On the flat screens stationed around the foyer I saw, as in a hall of mirrors, the bright flash of an armored personnel carrier erupting in a ball of flame on what might have been a road leading into a city in Iraq or Afghanistan, the lens capturing bodies and debris riding the explosive waves in slow motion.

Neither I nor anyone I loved or cared about had been anywhere near the trains that were blown up in Madrid back in 2004. One of the teachers I'd employed at the time claimed she knew someone who'd come down with flu the night before and missed her usual train into the city—and of course it was hit. Stories like this immediately became popular, and in the following week I heard variations on the theme over and over. Half the city had only narrowly escaped the attack. It became a sort of urban legend and a warning that the line between life and death is very fine indeed. It's an alluring prospect to think you've been spared for reasons beyond your comprehension, though for some this only confirms that existence is essentially chaotic. But for others it might serve as an inspiring invitation to get a jump on making some long-overdue changes—like back in Montreal when the *Challenger* exploded on live television.

For a week or two the Atocha attack was all the

shock I needed to remind me of what really mattered. A tragedy of that size put your own troubles into perspective. I booked time for us with a marriage counselor, whom we visited for a few months, and on weekends we took Ava up into the sierra whenever we could. I tried to look past the neutral smiles, the rush to get home before a certain hour. I believed we were on the mend, drilling back down into the bedrock of our past. At the time it had seemed a hopeful exercise. I thought these trips might remind us about some of the good things, starting with why we'd fallen in love in the first place and how we used to invade one of the restaurants or bars in the village square with old friends and spend the day exploring the area. There were trails cut everywhere in the pine forests. We'd spend the weekend up there, and in the deep blue light that fell between the trees Isabel and I would separate ourselves from the group and find a perch that afforded a view of the town below and the wide grey mountains on the other side of the valley and wait for the hawks to appear, three or four at a time, cutting their wings against the sky. At the end of the afternoon we'd all pile into the cars again and drive down to José's big stone house in the village one over from Isabel's and there grill lamb chops and drink out in the garden until well after dark.

I know now that trying to go back to some better time is doomed to failure. You can never really turn back the clock. But the drives up into the pine forests all those years later, in the spring of 2004 while I was setting up the Dublin school and the Atocha station still smoldered, were a powerful tonic for me—even though part of me understood that those family weekends together were nothing but a rolling last hurrah.

After the movie I took the boys around the corner for a bite to eat. We ordered, then I stepped away from the table and called Madrid. It was four in the morning over there, but this wasn't the first time one of us had pulled the other out of a restless sleep. I held the phone against my ear and heard the overseas ring. An urge to call would come every so often and usually I was able to fight it off, yet for some reason I couldn't that night. What seized me now was the need to hear Isabel's voice and to know our daughter was sleeping safely in the room next to hers, which for years had been ours, and that somehow the small space that had contained our lives together was still intact.

"No, nothing's wrong," I said when Isabel asked why I was calling at this hour.

"Aye, *cariño*," she said, and gently hung up the phone.

After the boys were asleep that night, I listened to a message on the machine from their dad. When I called back he picked up in Naples, Florida, with a yelp of professional enthusiasm.

"What is it down there, seventy degrees?" I said.

"Some guys have all the luck, right? I guess that's me!"

He was sitting across the table from a well-known baseball player, four drinks into a big night. I told him

I'd taken the boys to a movie; at least they'd enjoyed themselves. Hearing excited, lubricated voices behind him, I imagined cockatoos drowsing on low, moss-bearded branches and large athletes wearing fat gold rings.

"We signed the sweetest free-agency deal today," he told me. "We ate those assholes for lunch."

Envy and pity flooded through me after we hung up. He had the freedom that I'd longed for, that we all hoped for while waiting for our children to grow up, the freedom that, when it finally comes, feels more like a burden of lost opportunity than anything else. I wondered if he just didn't care anymore, or if he ever had. Did he know something that I didn't? Would his sons simply not remember his indifference? Would they care at all? Would those difficult months and years of his absence not matter in the end? I walked downstairs and poured myself a drink and drank it slowly, standing alone in my kitchen.

I was just back from a bike ride one Tuesday morning in May—one of the first warm days of spring—when a Skype request came up from Ava, which sometimes popped up at the strangest moments. I was drinking a glass of orange juice and watching the laptop I kept open in the kitchen whenever I was home.

"Hey, Daddy," she said.

"Peanut," I said, leaning into the screen. "What's up? How are you?"

"You look silly."

I was still wearing my cycling gear, including my helmet.

"Guess what," she said with a great big smile.

"Tell me."

"Mom said I can visit you this summer."

I cycled to work that morning, like a man reborn, my heart exploding. I'd already started making plans in my head—places I'd show her, things we'd do together. I turned a fresh eye to the city for the first time in months. The sunshine was warm, and a thin line of clouds sat benignly on the farthest horizon. The trees on the front lawns and parks I passed were budding out, their leaves pressing into the air like little green wings.

Later the same afternoon Holly Grey broke the silence between us with a phone call. "It's me, Charlie," she said. "How are you? Is this a good time?"

As we spoke, I began to believe she was calling for more than the reason she eventually presented, which was to invite the four of us to a barbecue one Saturday afternoon in June. I told her that sounded like a good idea, and she named a few dates. I wrote them down and told her I'd ask my brother if he'd like to join us. But I believed I heard something else in her voice. Did she want to talk about who we'd been and what we'd once had? Why I'd left her hanging like that all those years ago? Were there any feelings left? I thought these questions hung between us now as we spoke and that the excuse of this barbecue was only an occasion to answer them.

"Touch football in the yard," she said. "Some burgers. Totally casual."

"Perfect. The kids'll have a great time. I'll look at these dates and get back to you."

I didn't tell Hilary about this phone call or where I was going with Nate and his boys, and I drove out there three Saturdays later.

The truth was I didn't know what to expect, but the fantasy of starting up something again was, in the light of day, little more than a pleasant daydream I dipped into from time to time. I was more aware than anyone that life rolls on, people change and the circumstances that separated us were wider and more telling than the past we shared. Holly's kids, as if to remind me of this fact, were shooting baskets in their driveway when we pulled up to the house sometime around three that afternoon.

It was close to the middle of June now, and the sun was high and the streets were filled with a brilliant clear light. Riley was wearing cutoffs and a maroon Harvard T-shirt, the sleeves rolled up over the shoulders. Luke, shirtless and smiling, fist-bumped the boys and shook our hands. "Good to see you guys again," he said.

Riley's long chestnut hair was loose and sweaty, and small lines of perspiration traced down the front of her shirt between her breasts and under her armpits. She was the image of her mother in the pictures I'd seen of her when she was that age.

"Looks like you're getting a real workout," Nate said, shaking her hand. "That's good to see, kids keeping fit."

She smiled, the basketball tucked under her arm, and that's when I first noticed a habit of hers that surfaced often that day—holding the tip of her tongue against the back of her front teeth, her mouth parted slightly, when she smiled.

In a moment Holly and Glenn came around from the other side of the house, both smiling broadly. "We were starting to wonder!" she said, holding a small gardening shovel in her gloved hand.

"Good to see you both," Glenn said.

She looked great, of course, and when I went to shake her hand, she said, "Oh, right!" and kissed my cheek. She smelled like the bright day and the soil she'd been turning and the vaguest scent of perfume or bath soap, and as I breathed in, I felt the same nervous wonder that had taken me last fall and feared that my face and eyes betrayed my nervousness and longing.

"The kids are excited about being here," I said. "This is a good idea—getting together like this."

Glenn nodded with a smile. "We should've invited you earlier. We had to get through that winter first, but Holly's been talking about reconnecting for months. Faces from the past."

"It's true," Holly said, not at all defensively. "I kept wanting to call. Come. We'll get you a drink and show you around."

As they led us to the far side of the house, out of earshot of where the kids were playing basketball on the long sloping driveway, I tried to focus on the moment—Glenn was to my right pointing out some feature of the house he thought I'd find interesting—but I couldn't help watching Holly as she walked ahead with my brother into the side yard. The old white dress shirt she wore was tied in front at the waist, and the faded jeans that hung loosely off her hips hinted at a figure that had hardly changed in the past twenty years.

With drinks in hand, they showed us the work they'd done on the garden just that day, naming flowers and vines and filling us in on this neighbor and that and the charms of small-town living. Nate pitched in, keeping the conversation going. Seeming pleased to be sipping a cold gin on a hot day in the company of an attractive woman, he kept offering up compliments on the garden and the house, a redbrick Victorian that sat squarely in the middle of a generous corner lot. As the afternoon rolled forward, I began to suspect that I'd been well off the mark in thinking that Holly had some ulterior motive for asking me here. That everything suggested she was perfectly happy served to confuse my sense of balance. I didn't know whether I felt impressed or saddened that here in front of me were two people who actually *gardened* together on weekends. They were one of those rare couples who still did things together. With two kids and a man she enjoyed spending time with, it looked to me like she was making a real run at happiness. She'd chosen right, something few of us could claim to have done with any honesty. I watched as her husband spoke—talking about the trouble they'd been having with the aphids this season—and followed her eyes and mouth for any sign to the contrary; and when none came I felt foolish and relieved and disappointed all at once. And so I dragged myself back into the middle of a fine day while they gamely carried on.

They led us around to the front of the house and up to the wraparound porch, which had heavy colonial pillars and a grey plank floor and overlooked the quiet tree-lined street. Glenn went inside to refresh the drinks, and when we settled in he told me and Nate what had drawn them here in the first place, back in the midnineties. Things hadn't changed that much since. It was still on the small side and charming; even now, he said, the Anglican church rang its bells every Sunday morning, the farmers' market kept its regular weekend hours, and along the banks of the modest river cutting through town you could still see kids eating an ice cream or paddling a canoe on a summer's day.

"And you, Charlie?" he said. "I guess you're over the culture shock by now?" He took a sip of his drink and set it on the table between us.

"I've been too busy to notice," I said, exaggerating only slightly. "There've been some changes, anyway. I was just a kid when I left."

"I'll bet. Twenty years in Madrid's a long time. Holly tells me you've got a daughter."

"More Spanish than the siesta itself."

"You must miss her," he said.

"In fact, she's coming over next month."

"Excellent."

"It's taken some planning," I said.

"Some arm-twisting, more like it," Nate said.

"Niagara Falls, the CN Tower. The whole bit. I'm giving her the whirlwind tour. Pulling out all the stops."

"And your ex-wife is over there?" Glenn said.

"That's right," I said.

He nodded serenely.

"There's so many things you can do when she comes over," Holly said, leaning forward in her chair now, hands on her knees. "Maybe we could get the kids together."

"That might be a nice idea," I said.

"He's booked some time at the cottage," Nate said.

"You've got a cottage?" Glenn said.

Nate named the lake, which Glenn, raising his glass again, said was great for bass and muskie. "Cottage living," he said. "That's a real vacation, if you ask me."

"She's never been here, right?" Holly said.

"First time."

"Oh, she'll love it here," she said.

"It's like a first love," Glenn said, looking at me and Holly, "seeing a new country. The impression lasts forever, right? She'll have a great time."

It was a simple observation about first love, but I understood by the way he smiled and looked at us both, and by the slight shudder that seemed to pass through Holly, that Glenn had never heard of Miles Esler.

"No pressure there," I said. "But let's hope it's a positive inauguration."

So she'd never told her husband about the love of her life. As the conversation regained its footing from that strange stumble, I wondered how such a thing was possible. How do you live with someone all those years and keep something like that separate and hidden like some ugly secret? Glenn had no idea about a time when his wife knew with absolute certainty the boundless freedom of being in love for the first time. Or had I misread him? On that afternoon I didn't believe I had. Was this a memory she needed to protect from retelling in order to keep it intact and pure? I could think of no other reason. And then, as I rolled my glass between my palms, I noticed that Nate was no longer sitting with us.

I excused myself and found the three boys glued to the Xbox upstairs in the sunroom. "You guys seen Nate?"

When they shrugged, I continued down the hall and found him propped up against Riley's door frame in the same pose my old roommate from Montreal used to hold when he talked about taking me out to get laid.

"Private party?"

"Speak of the devil," he said, turning.

"We're missing you downstairs."

Riley was sitting on the floor in her bedroom, leaning back on her hands. Her tongue was pressed gently up against her teeth, her mouth open slightly, as if she had a cold and couldn't breathe through her nose. Her jeans were sliced horizontally, purposely and expensively, down the long length of her thighs.

"You dated my mom in university. And you actually lived together in Europe? I think that's *so* cool."

"A hundred years ago," I said.

"I've never met one of my mom's old boyfriends before."

"I don't think there's that many of us out there."

She smiled and rolled her eyes. "No *kidding*!"

"Riley's practically got a gymnastics scholarship wrapped up," Nate said, and he almost looked proud. "I was telling her about Syracuse. They've got a lot of good sports programs on offer."

"The only problem being that it's in Syracuse," I said.

"It's a good town," Nate said, turning back to her. "Don't you worry about that. I had an *awesome* time down there. You'd love it. Friendly people, nice campus."

"Cool," she said. Her face was as bright as a cherry. "You two don't look much like brothers."

"I doubt it myself on occasion," I said, putting my hand on Nate's shoulder. "Walk with me," I told him.

I was annoyed that he'd slipped away to flirt with Riley—whether he knew it or not, that's exactly what he was doing. But it didn't occur to me that it could go any further than that. I just let it slide.

Ten minutes after we stepped back onto the front porch, Glenn fired up the barbecue, and soon the steaks and hamburgers and salads were brought out to the side yard. The patio table was set, and the kids came down, and as the day rolled into a long gentle evening and the light softened into a warm shimmering glow over that unsuspecting town, we all dug in and ate and toasted old and new friends alike.

✦| Ten

The notion that Ava had come over to have a look at my new life as much as to actually spend time with me was never far from my mind once she arrived. She wanted to know what had changed in my circumstances, and I was eager to show her that very little had, at least where it concerned her. On the surface my life here would seem as strange to her as it felt temporary to me. More than once I explained that Toronto was only a way station, and I had no intention of staying longer than necessary to get the academy off the ground. I'd long since focused my ambitions in five-year intervals and mapped out with relative certainty the shape of the modest empire I aspired to build. One day I'd have schools in Japan and South Korea. But I couldn't say I had the same sense of control and determination about my personal life. Looking ahead by increments of thirty days was difficult enough. Five years was simply inconceivable. But I knew there was no future for me in a city without my daughter.

I collected her at the airport on a Thursday in July, close to a year since I myself had come over, and the following morning, after an early night, Nate and the boys came by the house to pick us up.

"The señorita! This can't be the señorita!" he said,

walking up the front path, arms open wide. We were standing on the porch, cereal bowls in hand, blinking into the sunshine.

"I'll bet *you're* my uncle," she said.

He took her in his arms and gave her a welcoming hug. Titus and Quinn lurked shyly behind.

She liked him immediately, of course. What wasn't there to like? He was enthusiastic, confident, friendly, solicitous.

"This one's riding shotgun today," he said.

We had planned, perhaps too typically, a drive out to Niagara Falls that morning. It was just the first of many excursions I had organized for Ava. The academy was up and running well enough now that I could take some time off. I'd keep her busy and hopefully any interest she had in this country might deepen, some connection would form, a reason to return again and again would present itself. I had hoped a visit to this natural wonder might make her father's home seem a northern paradise where such marvels abound. An adventure that would later be talked about in Madrid, it was our Taj Mahal. I'd first seen the falls myself when I was a boy and spent an hour lost and wandering through the park looking for my parents. When they found me, Nate punched me in the shoulder and told me not to get lost again. I remember very little other than that. Ava was still free of the wearying irony that dripped from the pores of the hypercool teenagers I dealt with at work every day now. I believed (or hoped, at least) that she might feature this in the mental brochure we keep of family destinations.

"Shotgun?" she said, unfamiliar with the idiom. "What's that?"

"It means the Three Stooges ride in the back."

He kept up the shtick—that she was some sort of prize, an object of reverence—for most of the day. At Niagara the kids tramped over the park green as a pack of three while Nate and I strolled behind, cameras slung over our shoulders. We got hot dogs and watched the cataracts from the vantage point of a picnic table set back against a stand of willow trees. It was an easy day. The falls were inarguably a sight, and they held the children's attention for longer than I could have hoped. Later the five of us stood at the railing and watched mountains of water slide into the abyss. By virtue of age Ava seemed to take on the role of the leader, a part that was new to her, as far as I could tell, but seemed to please her. Though the boys had no idea what it meant to come from a country as little known to them as Spain, her sudden and mysterious appearance in their lives made them—Titus especially, I think—expand their sense of horizons. Until then neither had seemed much interested in the place I'd lived for the past twenty years. As we strolled up Main Street looking for the wax museum that afternoon, the three of them stopped and coalesced in front of a storefront window twenty paces ahead of me and Nate. The boys stood on either side of Ava staring at her finger, which was pressed against the glass. To me at that moment she looked disturbingly and marvelously like a young woman. Quinn turned to us and said, "It's a map of the world. We've found where she lives! We've found Spain!"

I introduced Ava to Hilary a few days after the trip to Niagara Falls, and on the strength of an evening that went better than I'd anticipated, I took the chance that my daughter and girlfriend might actually enjoy each other's company and floated the idea of a night or two up at Nate's cottage.

"The one in the book you showed me?"

"That's the one," I said.

It was all blue water and pine trees ringing the wide circle of the bay when we pulled in that after-noon a week or so into the visit, and ten minutes later Ava was standing on the dock in her bathing suit and looking at the lake and nodding with approval. I came down and stood beside her. She'd never seen anything like these northern forests and lakes we'd passed on the drive up here.

"Look at that hill of trees on the other side," she said. "It's like a dragon's back, how it narrows down to the neck and goes up again where his head is?"

"I see it," I said.

"This is amazing."

"So what do you say, you going in?"

"Well, yes!"

"Okay then."

She jumped in, swam out to the diving platform, climbed up the ladder and called for me to come in, too. I went up to the cottage and got into my bathing suit and came back down a minute later and met her at the tire swing. The rope was tied to the biggest branch of a tree that leaned out over the water. She grabbed hold, and I got the swing going in wide swooping arcs, and after a few hesitations she launched herself and swam through the air, arms and legs going like mad, and slapped heavily against the surface. After three or four tries she got the hang of it. She'd come up with a joyful shriek and call out that she wanted to do it all over again.

When I saw Hilary standing on the dock a few minutes later, I thought maybe I had everything I wanted and needed. Ava was having the time of her life, and this smart woman who looked terrific in a bathing suit wasn't threatened in the least that I was a dad first and foremost and the kid I loved meant more than anything else in the world to me. If Holly at that moment had paddled by, I wouldn't have even noticed. Or that's what I told myself, anyway. For the first time in too long I was staring at my future, and what I saw filled my heart like it hadn't been in a long time.

I threw Hilary a smile from where I stood by the tree, pushing the rubber tire Ava had crawled into again, and she smiled back as she slipped into the water and swam toward the diving platform. I turned my attention back to my daughter and gave her another good push, and Hilary went past the platform out into the middle of the bay. She grew smaller and smaller until she looked no bigger than an otter and then disappeared around a bend into the wider lake.

We played on the tire for another twenty minutes at least. Then I went up to the cottage to put lunch together and brought it down on a tray. We sat on the dock and ate sandwiches and drank iced tea and enjoyed the views and the sunshine, and Hilary was gone a good hour before I started worrying that something had gone wrong.

I pulled the canoe out from the crawl space under the building and carried it down to the dock and set it in the water, then got two paddles and a life jacket and helped Ava into the canoe, and ten minutes later we were out in open water.

Ava had never been in a canoe before but seemed to like it. "You think she's okay, right?" she said.

"Yes, I do. We're just having a paddle here."

By now I was thinking it was a mistake to come out this far with Ava. I should have just called some emergency number, if there was one. What if we tipped over or found Hilary struggling, or worse?

And that's when Hilary's head appeared again, a dot on the horizon. At least I thought it was Hilary, though it was too small for me to be sure. But as we got closer, I saw her lift an arm and wave, and we heard her voice traveling over the water.

"Ahoy there," she called.

She was smiling and radiant when she came up alongside the canoe. "There's an island just around there," she said, pointing. "An island of wild blueberries!"

"Jesus," I said.

"You weren't worried!"

"Are you some sort of Olympic swimmer or something?" Ava said, smiling.

Hilary let go of the gunwale and swam under the canoe and appeared on the other side. "Nope. Just a happy fish."

After a late supper we went down to the dock to watch for falling stars. The sky was clear and dazzling, and the loons were hidden out there on the black water and calling to one another in a lonesome, plaintive way that made me feel happy and connected to the night. The three of us lay out on the warm boards, waiting for something in the sky to move. One came almost right away, but then for a long time the only thing we saw up there was the clumsy track of a satellite cutting the dark at its snail's pace. We didn't talk for a long while and just lay there peacefully, the anxiety of that scare out on the water that afternoon long gone.

"Silence," I said.

"Isn't it beautiful?" Hilary said.

"It is. That's the answer, right?" I said. "It's silence."

At the Falls, leaning against the handrail watching the water disappear over the gorge, Ava had dangled one of her brainteasers under my nose. *What's broken every time it's spoken?*

Sprawled out on the dock, the three of us still looking skyward, I felt Ava's arm tuck into mine. *"Muy bien, Papá,"* she said quietly, still watching the stars.

Then, again, the silence.

. . .

Next day I went down to the water with a fishing rod and took a few casts into the lily pads. Ava was already down there reading cross-legged on the dock. The water was dead still, and bands of mist snaked over the surface and rolled upward in small vanishing leaps. The light was new and fresh, and the heat of the day hadn't yet gathered.

"There's no fish in here," I said, flipping the rod tip forward.

She turned a page.

I took a few more casts watching the lake. "But it sure looks nice," I said.

This went on a little longer, then Ava folded the book over a finger and looked at me with an annoyed smile.

"Good book?" I said.

"You know you two don't have to sleep in different rooms just because I'm here."

I had no idea whether she'd been brooding about this all morning or the thought had only just then jumped into her head.

"We're taking things slow," I said.

"I'm almost thirteen, Dad. I *know* what grown-ups do when they're alone together."

"You do, do you?"

There was a pause.

"I mean other than argue," she said.

"Your mother and I barely ever argued," I said.

"Yeah, right. Maybe not with your voices," she said, opening her book again.

Near the end, the freeze-out between me and Isabel was as loud as any shouting match. Ava knew this better than anyone, of course. I remember being conscious that things were unraveling quickly, but at the same time not quite believing it. Out of optimism or perhaps ignorance, I held on to the idea that things would right themselves between us—that just ahead on the horizon was some natural watershed we were approaching and that the best plan was to keep a steady course and ride forward until the landscape forced the issue. I didn't know what role I'd have in that happening other than offering dogged perseverance and patience. But patience in a man's world is little more in a woman's than circumvention and avoidance.

Ava turned another page.

"Maybe we can take the canoe out later," I said. "Or go for a hike. We could follow the road around the lake. Check out that dragon on the other side."

"Don't treat me like a child, okay?" she said.

"You said that yourself, how it looked like a dragon over there."

She fixed me with an annoyed and pitying stare. "Everything looks like whatever you want it to look like if you're far enough away. That's why you're here."

I couldn't argue the point. Somehow she'd gotten into my head. "But I'm coming back," I said.

"No, you're not. You're just running away. You *and*

Mom. You're both stupid selfish idiots with your new Pablos and Hilarys."

She didn't say another word to me for the rest of the day. She could barely even look at me. She just sat in the shade under a tree and read her novel and then, after a tense supper, shut herself in her bedroom. I'd told Hilary what was going on, and after the lights in Ava's room finally went dark around eleven, we stood out on the deck and shared a cigarette. I felt like all the life had been kicked out of me. I'd never heard that kind of anger from my daughter before and kept hearing it in my head, over and over. *Stupid selfish idiots.* And she was right. You can't get mad at your kid for calling it like it is.

"You're thinking about going back, aren't you?" Hilary said, handing me the cigarette.

"I always am. How could I not?"

"Looks like it's decision time."

"It's always decision time when you have kids," I said.

"It'll be all right," she said.

"Sometimes it feels like I've spent Ava's whole life just waiting for her to grow up. And now she's half out the door, and I can't do anything about it. That's no way to spend your life, is it? Just waiting for your kid to grow up?"

The night air was cool, and the lights from the cottage windows shimmered over the grass and the silvery fingers of the beech trees. The lake was lost in darkness, and the night was deep and still, and all I wanted to do was swim out into the middle and let myself sink to the bottom.

"No, it's not," Hilary said, "though this isn't exactly my area of expertise."

"I wouldn't say it's mine, either. You can probably see that by now."

"You shouldn't beat yourself up."

"I don't know a lot of men who gave it much thought before it happened. Having kids. And then you're in the middle of it, and you're dealing with it, people changing all around you."

Voices came through the dark from the opposite shore, joyful and relaxed, people celebrating a fine night up north. I couldn't make out the words, but they were the sounds of summer by the water, notes of celebration and renewal.

"I suppose it serves me right," Hilary said.

"What's that?"

"Your heart's going where your daughter is. Every time. You'd be an asshole if it didn't, right?"

"I'm a dad before anything. At least I know that much. But I thought maybe it would be easier. Coming over here, I mean. I thought maybe everything would be easier."

"I think that's why I'm starting to like you," she said, taking the cigarette from between my fingers. She took a puff, then flicked it over the railing. "I'm not keeping you here. As long as you know that."

We got ready for bed after that. While Hilary used the washroom, I stayed in the kitchen and watched a moth bouncing off the ceiling light.

"You *do* know this separate-room thing is silly, right?" she said when she was done. Her mouth tasted like toothpaste.

"I know it is," I said.

"But I guess it's kind of sweet, too."

I switched off the kitchen light and climbed miserably into my cold bed at the end of the hall, my daughter's words still ringing in my ears. I listened to the lake and the voices and the bounce of a springboard echoing through the night and thought about the days when I used to push Ava in a stroller down into the heart of the Retiro Park, watching the fortune-tellers reading palms and flipping tarot cards. I never stopped to hear my fortune but always wondered what lay ahead for us, where we'd be in ten or twenty years and what the little kid in the stroller I was pushing was going to end up being like. It was different every time I thought about it, but I never imagined her giving up on her parents like she had this day at the lake.

⇥ Eleven

I looked up and saw Holly talking to the receptionist at the front desk. It was Monday in late August now, and I was on the phone organizing some meetings in Dublin and Madrid for the following Friday and Saturday. I told the person on the other end of the line that I'd call back and went out to meet her.

"You're busy," she said. "I guess I'm barging in."

"No, no," I said, "this is great."

I led her to my office and closed the door behind us. She took a seat in the chair across from my desk, her back to the window looking out over College Street.

"What's up? This is a nice surprise."

"I was in town. I just dropped Riley off at a friend's house. She's going to a concert tonight. I thought I'd say hello."

"Good. I'm glad you did."

We hadn't spoken since the barbecue. Now she made a show of turning her head and checking out the office. "It looks great. A lot of work, I'm sure, but it has a good feel."

"I was having my doubts there for a while that we'd actually see the day it was done."

"You've got something to be proud of."

"Thank you," I said.

"And your daughter? Ava, right? You said she was coming?"

"Been and gone. A few rough patches. But we managed. Just working out the new situation. It's tough for kids."

"For parents, too, right?" she said.

I wondered if she was here to tell me that she and her husband were splitting, that he'd picked up on something between us and got her talking about the past he never knew she had. I didn't know what to think. But it seemed she had something to tell me.

"Do you ever think about those days back in Montreal?" she said.

"It was a pretty intense time. Sure, I do. A lot, actually."

"Sometimes I can get pretty nostalgic," she said.

"When I saw you last fall—I don't know how to say it. It really took me back. It was great. I felt great. Confused but great. It was nice to be reminded that we had that in our lives."

"It's nice to hear you say that," she said.

"It was pretty tough when I first got over here. What do you do when you're uprooted, right? You look for something to hold on to. And there you were."

"You're saying nice things," she said.

"I guess I am. But it's true."

"I don't really—" She stopped herself.

"I think I know what you're going to say."

She shook her head and motioned with her hand that I should give her a minute.

"Okay," I said.

And so I sat there waiting quietly for her to tell me that her marriage was over and that she'd been thinking about us and that maybe, once she got back on her feet again, maybe we could start slow, little by little, and see where we were. That's why she'd come. I saw the confusion of a failed marriage in her face and felt sorry and pained that I couldn't help her heal her broken heart any faster than the slow, agonizing time it would take.

"Miles jumped," she said.

For a moment I was taken aback, the pivot was so jarring. "We don't know that. No one can ever know that."

"I do," she said.

"You know he wasn't like that. He wasn't that sort of person. He was full of life. He wanted more than anything to—"

"I know he did."

"You can't say that," I said. "And you shouldn't say that."

"I told him I wanted to be with you." Her eyes began to tear up.

"I don't understand."

"I was a coward, Charlie. I was in love with you. And I didn't know how else to tell him. It just happened."

"You're telling me something I can't understand," I said. "This is too much."

"I told him after you fell asleep. We were lying in bed, and I said this horrible thing to him and just kept going and going and he didn't say anything. He didn't say a word. I thought he didn't care anymore. So I just kept going, taking him apart like that. And when I woke up he was gone."

I remember not knowing what to feel or say that afternoon, and in some ways I still don't. In less than a minute the last twenty years had been entirely recast, and the first love of my life was now grounded in the bedrock of a suicide. It was sadness I felt more than anything that day—I can say that now—but I felt angry, too. She'd wear that guilt forever, it would never go away, and there was nothing I could do or say about it to help her. Miles had died thinking the two people he loved most in his life had been laughing at him behind his back, and I couldn't change that, either. That world of our youth, so long a source of strength for me, was gone.

I'd sat there stunned, my head abuzz, trying to process everything she'd told me, and checked the urge to rebuke her, to tell her she'd killed one of the most beautiful human beings either of us would ever know. Eventually she rose, wiped the tears from her eyes and silently left me to the privacy of my own thoughts.

I went for a hard ride along the river that afternoon, needing desperately to move. To do something. People in the office were looking at me with worried expressions, so I dipped down into the valley and rode for as long as I could, hoping this would clear my head, and when I got back to the house I showered and changed and tried to eat something. My friend had died all over again. That's what I kept thinking. Suicide was an ending that never stopped. It went in circles, and the arc of its spirals grew wider as time passed, and you thought about it so much you had no idea anymore if you hadn't actually been there, hadn't in some way contributed to it or not done enough to keep it from happening. I couldn't stop thinking about it. I imagined what his last thoughts must have been—that the two people he'd loved most in his life had betrayed him. That was the last thing he knew, and it always would be.

That evening I walked over to Nate's house, as I often did when he was away, to see if the cats needed any food or water. Their bowls were full—it seemed they hadn't touched a thing. The older one, Mouse, appeared at the top of the landing. I climbed the stairs and picked her up and turned and saw Riley standing in the bathroom doorway in my brother's robe. It was hanging open. She pulled the folds together quickly, but not fast enough. It was obvious what was going on, even before Nate called out to her from his bedroom.

"How about that towel, angel?" he said.

Her face turned red, then she slipped back into the bathroom and closed the door.

The next morning I stood on his doorstep, sweating, my heart pounding madly in my chest. The image of

Riley in my brother's bathrobe had stayed with me the whole night. I'd tossed and turned and remembered Nate draping his arm around Isabel's shoulders years ago in Madrid and taking a wild swing at me in the street in front of that bar. But things were worse now than I ever could have imagined. I didn't know what to think anymore. The door opened then. He was smiling.

"The return of the better brother," he said.

"Is Riley still here?"

He was wearing sweatpants and a blue short-sleeve shirt and holding an unopened bottle—my present from the duty free, I was sure—in his right hand. A golf club was leaning against the sofa, and a coffee mug that he'd been putting into was turned over on the floor. Music was playing in the background.

"You expect me to kiss and tell? Here, go on, take it," he said, offering me the bottle. It was a Courvoisier Vieille Réserve. I didn't take it.

"Your kids are staying with their mother full-time now," I said. "They don't want anything to do with you anymore. You're a selfish prick. They finally see that."

He looked over my shoulder into the bright morning, then turned his eyes back to me. "You've gone over to the enemy, I see. I don't know why I'm surprised."

"You've only got yourself to blame, Nate."

"Just wait till your turn comes, brother. That's all I can say. When someone tells you Ava's through with you? Is that when the wounded little brother comes crawling back for help?"

"I'm not here to talk about my daughter," I said.

"Fair enough, then. Come on, for services rendered," he said, offering me the bottle again. "Think of it as a fee. You earned it. I wouldn't have had a chance with that sweet little piece of ass without your help."

I took it by the neck and looked at it, and when he smiled and turned around, I stepped over the threshold after him and raised the bottle in the air and brought it down on his head as hard as I could.

He dropped to his knees and made a strange gurgling sound and slowly raised his hand and touched his head. He gazed up at me with a look of confusion, like he didn't know who I was or what had just happened. Streaks of blood lined his face. He tried once to push himself up into a standing position but slumped forward and caught himself with his left hand against the sofa.

"Stay down," I said.

I helped him into a sitting position on the couch and held a cushion against his head.

"Just stay there," I said. "I'll make this simple for you. If you so much as *see* her again, a single phone call, a text message, anything, your kids will be visiting you in prison. I promise you that." Then I turned and walked back out into the sunshine.

→| Twelve

Three days later

I flew into Madrid via Dublin for Ava's thirteenth birth-day. It was Saturday morning now, that cat-and-the-comma riddle was still fresh in my head, and there was still no news about my brother. Walking to work, I peered into the café across the street from the academy. Along with a few other restaurants and bars, the Café Comercial was one of our landmarks, a place where Isabel and I used to meet once or twice a week to sip coffee and chase down each other's thoughts in a new language. Whenever I saw it now, I remembered us as we'd been long ago in a far less complicated time. I'd often stop and have a look inside and think about things, the past or maybe what lay ahead, and end up coming away with little sense that I was any wiser or better off than I'd been fifteen or twenty years earlier. And I'd peel myself from that window wondering if other people had those thoughts—that too many of life's lessons were hidden away somewhere in the past like a forgotten stash of unopened Christmas presents moldering away in a dark closet, no good to anyone.

Two young people were studying away at the table closest to the window. I could have laid my hand on their heads but for the streaked pane of glass between us. I recognized one, the girl, as a student at the academy. She'd been with us for years. There was a regular little home office spread out on the marble tabletop between them: a notebook and dictionary, two pens, coffee cups, a small yellow square of Post-its, saucers and spoons, empty sugar packets. After mistaking a stranger in the café for my brother, I started across the street to the Ocaso Seguros building, the most elegant in the neighborhood and home to my first academy, and pushed through the heavy door and stepped into the lobby. It was cool as a mountain stream in there, all marble and high ceilings. The old man at the desk nodded good morning. I rode the elevator to the fourth floor, waiting for the familiar ding of the bell, then stepped off the lift and padded down the long corridor to suite 4000.

Our receptionist came out from behind her desk and welcomed me back with a peck on each cheek. She was a young pretty woman named Rosa. That morning she smelled of nail polish and citrus and fanned herself lazily with a yellow notepad she'd scribbled all over in blue ink. Riding low in the heavy leather chairs we'd brought in last summer to give the lobby a warm, loungy feel were two sleepy-looking teenagers, buds plugged into their ears. "I see you're holding down the fort," I said.

She ripped the top leaf from the pad and handed it to me. *"Siempre trabajando,"* she said, and made some good-natured quip about being chained to her desk all day. I glanced at the note. My first meeting was running twenty minutes late. I slipped the paper into my pocket.

Half the city cleared out to make for the sierra or one of the coasts in August. Five of the ten classrooms were empty now, their chalkboards wiped as clean as the day they were installed. But the fall term started in October, just over four weeks away, and the lead-up to autumn kept the back office busy. I had appointments stacked throughout the day, starting with my Housing and Home Stay coordinator, who'd e-mailed earlier that morning with news that we were fourteen beds short for the Japanese contingent set to arrive at the end of September. After that I was meeting with reps and owners from the feeder schools in Milan, Edinburgh and Tokyo.

"You'll know where to find me," I said.

I walked down the corridor to my office and turned on the two fans facing my desk. I angled each in the direction of my empty chair, pushed the thought of my brother out of my head and got down to work.

Isabel called while I was in the middle of a meeting with the owner of the King's Crown School of Languages, operating out of Tokyo and Osaka. A tall, slim man, and vaguely Western looking, Kichirou Gifu jetted between European capitals at least once a year, drumming up business, tweaking and renewing contracts and generally putting a face on his brand. He'd come over to Toronto for the opening last January. The contracts between our schools had represented 16 percent of my revenue over the past four years. For someone in his early fifties he seemed to have more energy than a man half his age. Tomorrow, more or less around the time Ava would be blowing out the candles on her birthday cake, he'd be in Rome to do there what he was doing here. Today he was wearing a light blue dress shirt, khakis, a red necktie and black loafers.

"Please, please," he said, bowing his head and gesturing to the ringing phone on my desk.

I'd been expecting one of those two-minute post-game conversations that sometimes followed our family get-togethers. *How did Ava seem to you? Was she taking this okay? Did you notice anything unusual?*

"So what did you think?" Isabel said.

"Just that she takes great pleasure in stumping her parents with those brainteasers. Once we got that novel out of her hands—she seemed great."

A few hours later, late that afternoon, I took Kichirou out for a drink. We'd found those fourteen additional beds we needed for the group coming in from Tokyo, and now we sat at a shaded table on the terrace of the Pizzeria Maravillas, in a plaza near the apartment Isabel and I had shared back when we first moved in together and where, in fact, Ava was conceived. Kichirou pushed a pack of Marlboros across the table and adjusted his sunglasses. I helped myself but didn't light up until the waiter brought me a beer and a rum and Coke for Kichirou. The glasses were ice cold and sweating. We smoked and people-watched and tried not to talk about work.

"It's weird," I said.

"What's weird?"

"My mind's been playing tricks on me all day."

"Tricks?" he said, retrieving a handkerchief from his pocket and dabbing the beads of sweat from the bridge of his nose. He readjusted his shades, then returned the hankie to his pocket.

"I'm seeing my brother everywhere."

He was silent for a moment. "I've had that. Last year in Stockholm I had jet lag so bad I thought every woman I saw was Claudia Schiffer."

"That's my kind of jet lag," I said.

"It was hard getting back on the plane, that's for sure," he said.

Kichirou and I went out on the town whenever we visited the other's territory. Midnight in Tokyo or Madrid with your brain and body still hardwired into a time zone on the other side of the planet can be a soul-crushing ordeal, we'd both agreed. So the host usually compensated by taking his guest out and staying up late into the wee hours. I was prepared to do the same tonight if he asked me to, but an old friend of his was driving up from Seville to see him, and I was off the hook. It wasn't seven yet. I was looking forward to a sound sleep in my air-conditioned room at the Reina Victoria. First, I'd grab a swim in the hotel pool, then drink something cold up at the rooftop bar, and maybe flip through a magazine or newspaper. There was a nice view of the city from up there. After a civilized martini or two I would hit my pillow like a ton of bricks.

We shook hands on the sidewalk, and I hailed him

a cab, tapped the roof twice, then started down the shady side of the street toward my hotel. At the Gran Via I saw the giant digital display next to the McDonald's, the screen as big as a house and measuring the temperature in glowing red numbers—each the size of a grown man. Forty-four degrees, it said. Shielding my face from the sun with my briefcase, I waited for the lights at the zebra crossing, then continued back into the shade and down Montera Street to the Puerta del Sol, the heart of the city, where I turned left on San Jerónimo and weaved through the narrow streets to the Santa Ana Plaza.

Café tables were set up in the middle of the square, orange umbrellas angled against the evening sun. Sparrows were flying overhead in circles, and waiters were carrying drink trays and plates of food to the busy tables. The air smelled of olive oil and black tobacco—after all these years one of the most stirringly romantic aromas I know. Sitting alone at a table was an attractive woman wearing a red dress and leafing through a glossy magazine, her right leg crossed suggestively over her left. The elegant sandals she wore were the sort that laced partway up the ankle and shin. I walked over and cleared my throat. "Surprise, surprise," I said.

"*Que tal, guapo?*" Isabel said, lifting herself from her seat to kiss my cheek.

I pulled up a chair and flagged a waiter.

The dress was something I'd bought for her a few years earlier, an ultrafeminine one of a kind that showed some leg, cherry red with a frill just above the knees.

She'd put some effort into tonight, that was pretty obvious straight off. We hadn't been out on the town alone together in years, and as we sat here now I wondered why
she'd taken the trouble of doing herself up so beautifully and staking out this table in front of my hotel.
I'd heard nothing that suggested things had gone sour
with the constitutional lawyer.

"And Ava? Where's the little genius this evening?"

She, I was informed, was catching a movie just
down the street at the Cine Ideal with a friend and the
girl's mother, who'd make sure Ava got home safe and
sound.

The waiter came with a couple of gin and tonics,
and the sky turned from blue to apricot, then purple to
black, and the modernized streetlamps that were meant
to look like something out of the 1800s came on, and
the square was bathed in a warm glow. To my surprise,
we talked about my life as a single man. She'd never
shown any interest in what was going on over in Toronto,
apart from updates on how the business was faring.

"It's chugging along," I said. "Some ups and downs.
I guess it's something I'm getting used to."

"And the girlfriend situation?" she said. "Are you
happy?"

"I see you've got your spies on me," I said.

"Of course," she said, smiling.

"And what are you hearing?"

"You mean apart from the fact that she's a good
swimmer?"

"She is that," I said.

Sticking mostly to the ups, I told Isabel about my

life over there in distant Canada, a little bit about Hilary, and also Ava's cousins and the good people working for me now.

"I'm glad you're happy," she said.

"Things work out in the end."

I didn't mention the phone call from Monica or what my brother had done. I was looking forward to the party and didn't feel like spoiling the mood by dredging up what he'd just put me through. The air was finally starting to lose that sharp daytime heat, and we were having drinks in one of my favorite squares in the city, and the edge in Isabel's voice that I'd come to expect was softer and more welcoming now than it had been in years. I wondered if we'd come to the point where we could actually talk like normal people instead of getting all twisted up and angry over the smallest detail or confusion. We stayed there drinking and talking pleasantly until just after midnight. And when it was time to walk her over to Atocha Street, where cabs were always circulating, she linked her arm through mine and then, without my expecting it, she kissed my face, not in parting but for no reason I could imagine.

"What's that for?" I said.

"For a nice night," she said. "For two nice nights."

We walked for half a block without saying anything. I didn't know what had gotten into her, but I felt good about that kiss. It had sent a warmth flooding into me, I won't deny it. Still, some suspicion was mixed in there, too. I was considering asking how things were going with Pablo when she said, "I was never in love with him. You understand that, right?"

This comment took me by surprise. "Actually, there isn't much about last year that I do understand," I said. "But no, I didn't know that. It's something I've been meaning—" I wasn't able to finish the thought.

She dropped my hand, and before I knew what was happening she was striding across the street toward a taxi double-parked on the opposite side. The driver's door was thrown open, with a pair of legs sticking out. Two oversize sneakers, as garishly fluorescent as two flaming birthday candles, pulsated in the slashing glow of headlights.

Isabel reached in and grabbed hold of whoever was inside and yanked him out and upright. A junkie, most likely, he had a car radio and a carton of cigarettes pressed against his chest. More than that, he had fear in his eyes. He stood there for half a second, then dropped everything and disappeared up the street.

"Look at these people," Isabel said when I caught up with her. "Everyone just standing around watching like it's some sort of circus!"

She was right. A crowd had gathered, and no one was moving a finger.

"Let's just get out of here," I said.

I picked up the radio and the screwdriver the kid had used to jimmy the lock, and Isabel reached across and put the cigarettes on the passenger seat. I passed her the radio, and she tried to slip it back into the empty slot in the dashboard. "Come on," I said. "Let's get out of here. Don't worry about it."

The group of people pausing on their midnight stroll to check out what all the fuss was about split in two when a man suddenly pushed through them, walking fast and wearing an unpleasant scowl on his face. The owner of the taxi, obviously. No one else around here had half as good a reason to look as angry as he did at that moment. Heavyset with all his weight in his shoulders, he crossed the street like a man who knows someone's ripping him off and is going to do whatever it takes to stop that from happening.

When I raised my hand to slow him down, I saw this was the same cabdriver who'd driven me into the city the night before. Thinking it might help matters that barely twenty-four hours earlier I'd actually been a paying customer, I reached out to shake his hand. I don't know whether the coincidence failed to impress him, or he simply hadn't registered it, but he shoved past me and hauled Isabel out of the cab by the scruff of the neck. I put my arm around his head and pulled him off her, then he turned and hit me square in the face. It felt like I'd sprinted headfirst into a brick wall, everything in my sight line seeming to elongate and slant violently to the right when, for no reason I could tell, he slumped forward and dropped to one knee. Isabel, the car radio in her right hand, was standing behind him. She'd cracked him over the head with it. I saw that stub of a finger when he put his hand up against his skull, then sat back against the front wheel of his taxi and slowly closed his eyes.

⇥ Thirteen

Three weeks after I stole
that silver picture frame up in Santander, I walked into
a bicycle shop in Madrid and met Isabel for the first
time. I remember the outline of her face before she
turned and looked at me, the surprised smile, how she
pushed up from leaning against the counter, her arms
crossed over her chest.

José's shop in those days was small and cramped,
filled with mopeds and racing bikes and smelling of
grease and rubber from the tires and inner tubes hanging on the walls. Isabel was wearing jeans and sneakers
and a green Clash *Sandinista!* T-shirt, one of my favorite records of all time.

"*Hola,*" she said.

The expression on her face was shy but welcoming
enough to make me think she worked there, maybe
selling bikes on her way through university. She looked
the part, anyway, and held a book whose cover showed
an illustration of a human head divided into math-
ematical sections. "*Son muy buenos,*" I said, gesturing
to her shirt.

That I was a foreigner was apparent to her well before I opened my mouth, I'm sure, but I suppose my
terrible accent would have only driven the point home.

When I ventured that opinion, she flew off into some further observations I couldn't make heads or tails of. I think I might have caught some reference to Joe Strummer, but that was it. She looked at me expectantly when she finished speaking, like it was my turn now, which it was, then I said in my pidgin Spanish that I couldn't agree more and I was looking for a used bicycle, something very cheap. She listened patiently, a sympathetic smile forming in the corners of her mouth, and then called out to someone in the back room.

"But the people doesn't ride a bicycle in Madrid," she said, turning back to me, her English just good enough to understand.

"Nobody?"

"Nobody. Is dangerous," she said with a shy accent.

"But this is a bike shop, isn't it?" I said.

"Yes. Vespas. Mopeds. Tour de France. That kind."

She introduced me to José when he came up to the counter. He was tall and thin, my age, with short black hair and a stud in his ear, and almost two decades later he would give me some background on Pablo.

When she explained my dilemma, he raised a finger to let me know I should wait half a minute, disappeared and then returned with something that looked like it hadn't been ridden in twenty-five years. He bounced it on the concrete floor with a jarring thump.

"*Que tal esto?*" he said. *How's this one?*

I took it out for a test ride. The chain was rusted, and the handlebars and front wheel were crooked, pulling the steering to the left. It was the worst piece of junk I'd ever tried to ride. In ten minutes he straightened everything out and oiled the chain and made a few adjustments. I tried to give him some money, but he said the thing had been cluttering up his back room for years, and he was glad to finally get rid of it. Though I tried to insist, he wouldn't take my money and suggested as a compromise that I buy him a beer.

He put a sign up on his shop door saying he'd be back in ten minutes, then the three of us went across the street to the Estrecho Bar. It was a nondescript neighborhood watering hole with crumbling plaster walls and a bright, shining bar top.

"So what are you doing in Spain, anyway?" Isabel said.

I attempted a short Spanish version of the story that had brought me here, having gotten used to talking in what essentially amounted to shorthand. I've since decided that there's nothing like crawling among the fundamentals of a second language to focus the mind.

"And for how long?" she said, rescuing me in English.

"I don't know," I said.

"Long enough to want a bike, anyway," José said.

On the other side of the street a man stopped in front of the shop, read the sign and looked at his watch, so José shook my hand and wished me good luck in not getting killed on that bike.

"Looks like it's just me and you," I said to this beautiful girl.

"I can practice my English. I need to practice my English."

"Your English is great."

"Oh, yeah," she said.

"No, really. You're my official translator. You helped me with that bike. Without you I'd be bikeless."

"Bikeless?"

"Without a bike."

"Okay. Am I hired?"

"You're hired," I said, raising my glass. "But you'll have to help me with my Spanish, too."

After Isabel and I said good-bye, I rode through the city and down to the Retiro Park warmed by the thought that I'd actually had a good conversation with a cute Spanish girl and a friendly shop owner in a neighborhood bar, much of it in their language. Afterward, as I cycled, enjoying the sites and the warm evening sun, I was able for a few hours to forget about Holly and all the sadness I felt after leaving her, and then Carmen, and focus instead on that small, bright flame of hope. She'd laughed at a few of my jokes and stood there—sportingly, I thought—as I tried, in Spanish, to give her a sense of where I was from and my tastes in music and the books I liked to read and exactly what I was looking for when I came to Europe. It didn't seem to bother her when I admitted that I really had no idea why I was here, other than a book I'd read that took place in the hills north of the city, and that I might stay for a month or a year. I didn't mention Holly that afternoon, of course, or that I'd left Santander in the dark of night, and didn't until we finally started dating a couple of months later.

. . .

Those first few days in Madrid I stayed at a pension in the centre of the city near the Puerta del Sol. Every morning I picked up a paper and scoured the classifieds for an apartment. My guidebook described one neighborhood in the north end as bereft of any notable history and therefore an area to avoid. Believing the rents might be more affordable up there, I strolled around it one afternoon. I had some addresses with me and managed to find a few of the buildings they belonged to. At the third or fourth place I buzzed from the street, an American answered the intercom, then invited me up to have a look around.

It was a decent-enough place, two bedrooms, if modest by every standard you could imagine. It didn't even have a real stove, just a hot plate set on top of the kitchen counter.

I told him a little bit about myself, nothing important, then he said, "Okay, when can you move in?"

"There's just one hitch," I said.

"What's that?" he said.

So I explained that I'd been robbed up north.

"That's not good," he said.

"I guess I'm in a bit of a bind."

He sat down at the living room table and pulled a chunk of hash from his breast pocket and began drying it out with a lighter flame. He crumbled it into his palm, mixed it up with a pinch of tobacco, then rolled and lit the spliff and passed it to me after taking a hit.

"How much do you have?" he said, breathing out a lungful of blue smoke.

The flat was small and dark, and its carpets smelled of mildew and stale cigarette smoke, but I guessed it cost more than I could afford.

"Not much," I said.

I took a puff on the spliff and listened to the story of how this painter from Ann Arbor had showed up in Madrid three years ago without a peseta in his pocket. He'd been robbed on the night train coming in from Lisbon, he said, on Christmas Eve, no less, and forced to spend Christmas morning at the Chamartin Station hitting up travelers for handouts.

He was happy to have someone to talk to in his own language. I told him a little about myself and about Holly and life back in Montreal. I didn't know where I would go next, I said, or when, but Madrid seemed to have more than enough to keep me busy.

"Oh yeah," he said, smiling. *"De Madrid al cielo."*

"What's that supposed to mean?"

"Next stop, heaven," he said.

I didn't know at the time that this refrain was meant to describe the city's lasting impression on those who visited. People came from the outermost regions of the country, the argument went, and once they arrived they no longer wanted to go back to where they came from, such were its wonders. You stayed there, and there you died. From the provinces to Madrid, from Madrid to heaven.

I dug into my pocket and pulled out a handful of coins. "This is it, after I pay where I'm staying." It might have amounted to four hundred pesetas, three or four dollars.

When I placed the change on the table, one of the coins rolled off the edge and dropped to the floor. He picked it up and slipped it in his pocket. "This'll do for now," he said.

The next day I found the English-language bookshop highlighted by my guidebook as a hub of the expat community and posted my name and services as an English teacher on the bulletin board.

I remember the beautiful light in the sky over Madrid in those early days. It seemed deeper and bluer, somehow. Everything to my mind seemed richer. The world thrummed with possibility. As the approach of early summer brought those beautiful colors down over the city, on its buildings and over the wild greens in the parks I visited almost every day, the small windows facing the interior courtyard of my new flat shimmered with heat in the late afternoon, exactly when I got home after a day of tutoring. By mid-June I had half a dozen private students, enough to cover rent and basics, but still had plenty of time to wander down a new street if something caught my interest. Back at the apartment, I'd read and prepare for the next day's classes before going out again to explore the city by night, either alone or with my roommate. Between six and seven, for close to fifteen minutes, direct light entered the flat. I sat at the round black table where my roommate had gotten me stoned, and where I'd since taken to eating my solitary meals, and basked for a short while in this private sunlight. It was around this time I realized that I had lost the sound of Miles's voice in my ear. I couldn't remember what he sounded like. And even when I was thinking hard about him, or dreaming about him, he was a vague and partial presence, as impermanent as that sliver of light.

My roommate usually left the apartment early in the morning in order to claim his preferred location at the park where four or five years later I would find myself pushing a stroller and whispering desperate lullabies to my colicky daughter. He spent his mornings chalk-drawing Raphael and El Greco imitations on the sidewalk. In the afternoons he carried his supplies to the Plaza Mayor, where he sold caricatures of Ronald Reagan and John Belushi and Helmut Kohl. He made a pretty good living at this. It was the sort of hand-to-mouth existence that appealed to us then, and for a short time we mastered it.

I started dropping by José's shop once or twice a week. It wasn't too far from the flat, and I went back the first time to buy a combination lock and ask for a couple of minor adjustments on the bike. But the real reason for going in was Isabel, of course. I hoped I'd see her again.

If it was later in the evening, near closing time, José and I grabbed a beer at the Estrecho Bar. Sometimes Isabel happened to pass by when walking home from the school where she'd been doing her practice teaching. She was in the last year of a work-study program in early childhood education, with a focus on handicapped kids, at the University of Madrid. By then José had told me everything he could about her, principally, in my mind, that she was single and had been for more than two years. I liked the idea that she was in no hurry and was the sort of girl who didn't need a boyfriend but was willing to wait till she found someone who truly interested her instead of just filling the empty space beside her.

Her father, Santiago, ran a hair salon three or four blocks from José's shop. Orphaned during the Civil War, he had no schooling whatsoever but was a savvy businessman and an artist with a pair of scissors, according to José, who'd once brought his copy of *My Aim Is True* into the salon and asked if he could have a haircut like Elvis Costello's, a sort of pompadour that was heavy in front and skinned down to the bristle up the back. The old women in the neighborhood lined up for Santiago's latest stylings and for the flirtations that made their hearts flutter. He'd given his daughter not only his dark eyes but also the easy manner with people, a calm and reassuring nature, that I began to see and admire so much in her.

I'd visited the salon once or twice by then to pick her up for the language lessons we were using as our excuse to get together. At the salon her father had taken my hand and pressed hard and looked into my eyes with a smile and said that he was glad to meet someone like me because he loved his only child more than anything in the world and he could tell I was the type of boy who understood how a father would take any bad behavior against his daughter as bad behavior against himself personally, that he would gladly and without any hesitation run such a boy out of town if anything happened to his daughter and that it was a great comfort to him to know I was of the same mind on this issue and everything between us was clear and up front. I agreed that everything was perfectly clear and up front, and he slapped me on the back and explained to his customers that I was from Canada and teaching his daughter English, and the ladies with their heads half consumed by the beehive hair dryers I'd seen only in episodes of *I Love Lucy* glanced up from their magazines and smiled politely and welcomed me to Madrid.

When Isabel walked by on the sidewalk while José and I were catching up at the bar across the street from his shop, I'd race out and haul her back in for a drink, and soon after that my friend would come up with an excuse to cut out, and the two of us would stay and talk for hours. Sometimes she'd take me around the neighborhood. The old men sitting in cafés or leaning on their canes against a storefront would greet her by name and warmly cock their heads and offer me a handshake, and for an hour I'd feel the privilege one gains when walking with a pretty girl in a foreign city, like suddenly everything is possible.

José and Isabel introduced me to their friends one night at the height of summer. Ten or twelve people were gathered around a couple tables in a square. The guys shook my hand and slapped my back like we were childhood buddies; the girls kissed me and smiled like they knew something I didn't.

After we took a seat, Isabel leaned forward and whispered in my ear that I was a big hit with all her friends. I hardly believed this was true at the time, but what I distinctly remember now was the smell of her hair and her skin—summer heat and sweet perfume and the faint taste of tobacco and the hint of her father's salon. This was the first time I'd gotten close enough to smell these things, and it was rapturous. In a moment, she turned away, but I hung there like a man suspended, wishing she would lean back into me with some new whispers.

We dipped into a dozen bars and taverns that night, never staying longer than one drink in any of them. I'd never seen people move so fast before. Her friends filled me in on the basics of drinking in Madrid. They called themselves "cats," they said, always on the move. The whole city came alive at nightfall and didn't stop until dawn. They were all incredibly patient with my Spanish, each taking plenty of time with me and asking simple questions to help me along. At one point Isabel and I found ourselves separated from the crowd in a neighborhood where the view opened north to where that novel was set that I'd read up in rainy Santander. In half the bars in the city there were pictures of Hemingway having a drink; you just couldn't get away from him. For some reason I'd always felt a little embarrassed to see those photographs. But on that beautiful starry night as we stood side by side, I felt all the preconceived notions of Madrid dissolve, and suddenly the moment was ours.

"I'll take you one day," she said. "We have an old place there. It's not much. But we like it."

"Okay," I said, leaned in and kissed her on the mouth.

She smiled and covered her lips with her hand. "Come on," she said. "Let's catch up."

Had I just spoiled everything? I felt the thrill of that kiss burning inside me. But now I didn't know if I'd made a fool of myself by misreading every signal she'd sent me over the last month and a half. In an instant I was convinced that I didn't have a chance with Isabel. How could I have been such an idiot?

I didn't see her the following week. I wondered if calling her might be just digging myself into a deeper hole. Maybe I'd write her a note to explain that I hadn't understood what was going on between us and it wouldn't happen again. I didn't mention the kiss to José but started thinking about Holly again, and then Carmen, and all I could come up with were sad thoughts. While I tried to go about my business and stay focused, I couldn't dodge the conclusion that I'd ruined my chances with Isabel.

The following Saturday José brought me to a bar in the Old Quarter where the same crowd as the week before was meeting. Isabel was there and as bright as ever.

"Where have you been?" she said, giving me two lovely kisses. "You've got to get a telephone!"

"You look great," I said.

She hooked her arm into mine and led me around to her girlfriends, each of whom gave me that same smile again. They knew something that I didn't, but what was it?

Near the end of the night we found ourselves in a small, dark basement bar where the party was starting to wind down. José's wife, a Basque named Amagoya, had already left; they had a baby at home, something I still couldn't believe. But he'd stayed on, watching the old piano player and smoking his heavy black tobacco cigarettes. Tomorrow morning wasn't his shift, he said.

Tucking a strand of hair behind her ear, Isabel leaned forward and asked for a light.

"Sure," I said.

Those girlfriends were still treating me like I'd saved her life, and the guys were acting like I was a long-lost brother. I thought I was making progress, or at least hadn't guttered everything with that kiss. When the flame caught, I noticed she was missing a small piece of ear from her right earlobe.

"What happened there?" I said, pointing.

"Where?"

"The ear."

"*Aye, la oreja,*" she said, rolling her eyes in a funny-story sort of way.

"Seriously."

"A hungry student."

"What do you mean?"

"He bit me. *Me mordió.*" She gnashed her teeth.

"That's terrible," I said.

"*Hijo de puta,* more like it," she said, leaning forward and pulling the hair back from her ear again. "Two *puntillas.*"

"Stitches?"

"That's the word," she said.

It was a forty-five-minute drive up to the mountain town where they'd all spent their summers as kids. That night she made a promise again to take me there, and I was hoping it wasn't halfhearted. But she didn't forget and stuck to her word. We drove up there the following weekend and met everyone at a bar on the main street. After an hour we drove higher up into the hills, to El Escorial, and pulled three aluminum tables together on an outdoor terrace and drank iced coffees and then walked through the old streets and a few rooms of the monastery. We ended up back at the square where we'd started, had another drink, then Isabel and I got back in her car and drove to her family's chalet.

It was well after nine when we got there, the sky still blue and clear and thin wisps of feathery clouds touching the tops of the mountains farther north. The house, a modest three-bedroom stone building at the edge of town, was a beautiful old place, derelict, a nightmare to get back in shape, I thought, but it looked like something out of the last century and fit my idea of what a Spanish country house should look like. It was surrounded by bramble and wild, untended fields strewn with rock. There were no other houses around. She produced a key hidden under a drain spout, and once we got inside we threw open the shutters and windows to let in the summer evening. The big stone fireplace in the main room, cold and dark, radiated the heavy dull scent of burned-down firewood.

All of her friends had chalets up here in the sierra. After a long night at the *discoteca* I'd likely end up going back to José's place in the next village over and crashing on his couch. Maybe someone else's, I wasn't sure—but certainly it wouldn't be here. That's when Isabel took me by the hand, led me upstairs to her childhood bedroom and began undressing.

Do we fail love, or does love fail us? This was a question I couldn't answer, and still can't. But in a clarifying instant I was someone else now, rejuvenated by the tonic of new love. As Isabel slipped out of her clothes that night, the last of my sadness and regret slipped away from me, at least for a time. And that's all I could ask. I had worn it too long, had tried too hard. Now I was a young man raked from the coals of his first love and brought back to flame. At that moment there was nothing more important or thrilling or hopeful in my life than the body and soul of this perfect Spanish girl standing naked in front of me. *Oh, the supple and poetic world of the heart,* I could have called out. *Oh, the endless mystery of this body.* I was taken by even more fantastical flights that evening, and after we returned from these heights, we lay fuck-drunk and soaked and smiling on Isabel's childhood bed and watched the sky darken and the August moon move resolutely across the open window.

After midnight we walked into the village and found our friends at a *discoteca* that sat at the end of the road overlooking a shallow valley now set in deep darkness. We went in and drank and danced. They were playing that summer's big Spanish dance hits, great poppy music you couldn't sit still to. Our friends knew we'd just done what we'd both wanted to do since the first hour we met. They were happy for us. They'd seen it coming from a mile off, those girlfriends and their knowing smiles.

Later that night, standing side by side at the edge of that valley, Isabel and I saw the cluster of bright lights shining on the horizon. My arm might have been draped around her neck or hers around mine. "There," she said, "you can see Madrid."

"That's where you live," I said.

"You too," she told me. "You live there, too, now."

⇥❙ Fourteen

We spent twenty minutes in the back of a police car that Saturday night before our daughter's thirteenth birthday. One of the two officers on the scene went back and forth between us and the cabbie, taking statements. We gave him our side of the story. Who knew what the driver was telling him?

Eyes closed, he'd sat there leaning against the front tire of his taxi long enough for me to start worrying this might turn into something much bigger. The cop was there when he stood back up, and as they talked he was still pressing his hand against his head and looking over at us like he wanted to pay back some serious damage. Every minute or so he'd touch his hand to his head and glance at it to see if the bleeding had stopped. It looked like it had.

By then most of the crowd had been moved along. Now the regular flow of after-hours Madrid streamed by, hipsters and preppies and hip-hop teenagers and nicely dressed older couples touring from bar to bar for drinks and snacks and enjoying the nighttime break in the heat.

I had a cut the size of a quarter under my eye, but it wasn't bleeding, partly because Isabel had dabbed a thumb in her saliva and gently pushed it against the abrasion.

"What are the odds, right?" I said. "I get picked up by the same cabbie you end up clocking a night later."

"Sounds like an Almodóvar film."

"Maybe Fellini," I said.

"I just hope he doesn't sue us into the Stone Age," she said.

"I'm having a serious case of déjà vu," I said.

"Are you seeing double?" she said, getting in close to my face.

"No."

"You think we should go to emergency?"

"My head's all right. It's just that I bashed Nate on the head with a bottle last week. And then here you are doing the same thing to that guy with a radio. Isn't that weird? I mean, for two people who've never hit anybody in their life?"

"Why the hell did you do that?" she said.

So I told her about everything—Holly and Riley, what sort of man my brother had turned into and how I'd learned that the death of my old friend from my university days wasn't the accident I'd always believed it to be. I told Isabel all this as slowly and as completely as I could, and when I finished she asked me one quick question, which was if Ava had ever been left alone with Nate. When I told her no, she never had, she nodded and whispered, "Thank God," under her breath, then turned forward and looked out the windshield. She didn't say anything for a while after that, and I started to wonder if I'd crossed the line somehow, possibly telling her too much about what was happening back there. It was hard enough for me to digest. We weren't a couple anymore, after all. Maybe all this business about Nate and Holly and Miles was confirmation that everything I represented was just too complicated.

"I guess all that makes it sound like a hell of a year," I said.

"Maybe life always looks bigger when you look at it from a distance," she said. "Maybe that's the moral of the story."

"I'm thinking this story's fresh out of morals."

"I mean the way we look back at things. What are you going to do with all that? It's still part of you. And those people, too. Maybe that's the question you're going to ask yourself one day. I don't know. We're just sitting in a cop car watching the night go by."

And then, just as that confined space seemed to get smaller, enough to push us closer together and maybe even into each other's arms, the door on my side opened and this skinny-faced cop was leaning forward into the backseat like an overeager bellhop.

"Bonnie and Clyde," he said.

"What's the story?" I said.

"The story is you're free to go. As long as you stop beating up on defenseless cabdrivers. You see those people over there?"

A respectable-looking couple, it turned out, an older man and woman, had seen the whole thing and told all concerned that the woman in the police car, the Good Samaritan, had chased off the real thief, and all she'd done in bashing the cabdriver over the head was try to protect her husband from taking a beating he didn't deserve.

Now the cabbie gestured dismissively, making it clear he was done with us, that he'd be happy never to see the likes of us again, then climbed into his taxi and peeled off.

It was coming on two in the morning when we got home, by which I mean the place that used to be my home but wasn't anymore. I was feeling light-headed, and the evening was still swirling around inside me, full of new and unusual possibilities. We stood at the foot of Ava's bed for half a minute, quietly admiring the small lump of pajamas that was our sleeping daughter, and then walked quietly back down the hallway and into the kitchen, where Isabel wrapped a clean dishcloth around a bag of ice and held it against my face. The kitchen was dark except for the light in the hallway, but I could see the stress of the night in her eyes and two lines at the sides of her mouth I'd never noticed before.

"We've got a birthday party tomorrow," she said, adjusting the ice bag. "Does it still hurt?"

"I'm fine," I said.

She left the kitchen without saying anything more and came back a minute later with a couple Advils. I took them with a glass of water.

"Everything happened tonight," she said.

"Almost everything," I said, then took the ice from her hand and placed it gently against the side of her face.

"It's cold," she said, cupping my hand. "It's nice." She closed her eyes, and her lips parted, and I felt her breath coming slow and clear, passing over the coolness off the ice. "I'm not sorry we went through this year. I hated every minute of it. But I'm not sorry. Why do you think all that had to happen?"

"The choices we made," I said.

"It's just the way we are," she said. "We're just people making choices." She didn't say anything for a minute. "Tell me the worst thing you did over there."

"There's a lot of days I'd like to forget."

"Just one," she said. Her eyes still closed, she pressed her other hand against mine, pulling the ice harder into her face, then returned it to the cut under my eye.

"What about something I didn't do?" I said. "Does that count?"

"Okay. What didn't you do that you should have?"

"I didn't visit my friend's grave."

"There's time," she said, "always time," and took the bag of ice from my face once more, and we led each other to the bedroom, which smelled of soapy perfumes and her deep aroma on the sheets and pillows, and we undressed in the light of the August moon and shared the ice until our skin and the bedding were soaked through and small, unforgettable shudders leaped between our bodies like little sparks in the night.

. . .

Ava was sitting at the breakfast table reading one of those gargantuan novels when I shuffled into the kitchen the next morning.

She looked up with an expression of horror on her face. "What happened to you?"

For a second I had no idea what she was talking about. It was her birthday, her father had slept in his own bed for the first time in more than a year, and this is how she said good morning.

"Your eye. It's black-and-blue. You got into a fight!"

"You should see the other guy," I said, leaning in to give her a kiss.

I told her the story while I made French toast with cinnamon and a scoop of vanilla ice cream, her favorite birthday breakfast for as far back as I could remember.

"She did not!" she said. "Over the head? With a radio?"

"Oh, yes she did! You should've seen it. Down like a sack of potatoes. Don't mess with that lady, I've seen her in action."

"Did your father tell you?" Isabel said when she emerged from the bedroom a little while later. She gave Ava a hug and a kiss, then turned to me and put her hand on my face and got in close to look at the cut. She smelled like a garden after a light rain, like the woman I'd made love to last night for the first time in too long. "The man's a punching bag. Look at him!"

Morning sunshine was pouring through the kitchen window; the room filled with the smells of fresh coffee and maple syrup. Exhausted, feeling like I'd been run over by a mountain bike, I was the happiest man in Madrid.

"Dad told me the cop called you guys Bonnie and Clyde," Ava said, grinning. "You two are *so* not Bonnie and Clyde."

How she knew who they were was another wonderful mystery. As a family we leveled that stack of French toast, her mother and I putting all our attention onto Ava, and geared up for a great birthday party. I watched Isabel carefully, listening for an edge in her voice or anything that might register as the first sign of dawning regret. But I saw none. Were we back on track again, I wondered, or might this collapse at any minute? So far as I could tell, it was as if some invisible dam had burst, and now everything ahead of us was open and clear. Ava was going to start with the questions, too, ones she had every right and reason to ask. Are you guys suddenly together again? Or is this just one of those sympathy things? Why are my parents such helpless idiots? But no questions came.

We walked over to the Retiro, just four blocks away, and strolled past men selling beads and necklaces, their blankets spread out under the plane trees opposite the boating lake. The fortune-tellers and tarot-card readers were there as usual, and as usual I didn't ask. I'm not sure I would have wanted to know. We found a seat at a café and had something cool to drink and watched the crowds growing along the promenade.

Ava was happy because it was her birthday and we'd soon be in the car driving north and her dad had spent the night. It was the greatest birthday present she could have hoped for. She didn't ask a single question, and part of me was glad she didn't. I was afraid that her mother and I had just set a standard we couldn't possibly keep up. But here I was, home again and back in her life, and neither of us had the heart to explain that our troubles weren't so easily solved.

The big stone house where we'd always held the party had been in José's family for four generations. It was a handsome old building, too big for one person to keep up or to fill with new furniture—or anything new, for that matter. Overrun with wild grass and bushes, the yard was more than José could keep under control. Once or twice a summer the two of us took turns hacking at the growth with the old scythe we'd found in the shed, but it was never enough. In the garden there was an old-fashioned hand pump and cistern rimmed with blue and green and red tiles, that I'd never seen anyone take water from, and on any of the four stone walls that closed in the property we usually found a salamander sunning itself, which Ava always loved when she was little. There was a rail line just beyond those walls, and every hour on the hour the train rumbled past carrying passengers down into the heart of the city. It was quiet as a church up there except for the trains, and the birds and the crickets and maybe a neighbor's kid bouncing a basketball out on the road, and much cooler than it was in the city. José used to host his end-of-summer party up here before Ava came along, and we always gathered around the huge granite table set back under the pergola that dangled wild vines over our heads as we talked long into the late afternoon. The table sat more than twenty, and every seat was always filled. The food would keep coming—most of it prepared by José—for two or three hours. And then at some point, when Ava was four or five, her birthday party started absorbing this annual feast and slowly, over time, became the main event.

After unloading the presents the three of us passed through the side gate and joined the party, shaking hands and kissing cheeks. All the guests were already milling in the back and side gardens, waiting for the birthday girl. They were, for the most part, the people who years earlier had known well before we ourselves did that Isabel and I were going to fall into each other's arms. What they knew in particular was the look of two people who were crazy about each other and wouldn't let anything come between them. They were here now, of course, and smiling, but it was a different smile I saw on their faces that afternoon—one that seemed to recognize hard times and the effort we'd made to get back to where we were, which unbeknownst to them was approximately twelve hours into a sort of marital détente.

Ava found her grandparents sitting together in the shade of the pergola. Her face aglow, she wrapped her arms around them and whispered that her father had slept at home last night, that it looked like her mom and dad were back together again, and this was the greatest birthday present she could have asked for. Her grandfather looked at me and smiled a half smile and raised his finger, as if to say, *Give me a minute of your time.* And I remembered then the first minutes he held his granddaughter in his arms. He'd wept openly and deeply and cupped the back of my neck in his hand and pulled me into him, Ava still in the cradle of his arm and said, "Now you are with us completely, you hear? Now you are my son."

Santiago was not well these days. He was close to eighty and had a chest problem that caused Pilar, his wife of fifty-two years, to worry over and pamper him, but this condition he never talked about or acknowledged in my presence. His problems were his own and meant to be worn privately. Still, he would have something to say about my year away and this tentative reunion of ours. He told me that men like us who grew up without parents had to work even harder to keep our loved ones near. "*You and I do not have this luxury otherwise,*" he said in Spanish. Family was a conscious act of will, not a habit you simply fall into and take for granted; that was for the lucky ones. Ours was a reality that demanded moral courage and determination. "*There is no room for false pride,*" he said. "*You understand that, don't you?*"

After this talking-to, I took a turn through the yard looking for faces I hadn't seen in more than a year. A dozen adults, all friends of ours, were talking and laughing and pouring drinks. Their kids were everywhere, climbing the short trees, throwing water balloons, stealing cakes from the dessert trays. Now in our fifth decade, with kids and houses and all the problems that come to us at that age, youth's defining passages were long ended, and we were each who we'd always be from this point on. And as I turned these thoughts in my mind, I found a couple, dear friends of mine, sitting by the hand pump with the girl they'd brought from China only ten months earlier. She was a beautiful little thing dressed in a blue bathing diaper with a little red ribbon in her hair. They had tried to conceive a child for more than ten years and now were holding up objects and naming them in the girl's new language and smothering her in kisses whenever she got the Spanish words for them right. I sat with them for a time, watching this little miracle, then got up again and resumed my tour.

Isabel was pouring herself a beer at the drinks table set up in the shade of the chestnut tree in a corner of the garden. She'd traded in the red dress of last night for a simple grey blouse and beige slacks. Ava had braided her hair in a ponytail after breakfast. It was raised up off the back of her neck and gave her face a thin, narrow look.

"Here's to strange nights," she said.

"And stranger days."

She smiled, hopefully, and the train on the other side of the stone wall rumbled past. We waited for it to disappear down the track.

"I'm coming back," I said. "This is where I want to be."

"You know I'm not asking for anything," she said. "I didn't plan for last night to happen."

"I'm glad it did," I said. "But that's not why."

"Things happen for a reason," she said. "I guess we have to believe that. Maybe that's as close to religion as I'll ever get."

A few hours later, after a meal that was course after course after course, the birthday cake came out just as the sun was beginning to set. The whole party gathered around the table, and Isabel and I stood on opposite sides of our daughter, and everyone sang "Happy Birthday" and cheered, and all the cameras came out and started snapping. The candles flickered.

"Here's my wish," Ava said. When she smiled she didn't seem at all self-conscious about the braces on her teeth. I think she was too happy to notice. She turned to us, touched her chin with her fingers to make like she was really thinking, then blew out her thirteen candles with a big draining breath.

I was flipping through pictures of the party and snacking on salted peanuts on Monday afternoon, thirty-six thousand feet above the Atlantic Ocean, when the flight attendant brought me an apple juice. A pleasant-looking woman with light blue eyes, she smiled and leaned forward when she poured the juice into a plastic cup and placed it on the seat-back table.

"Now that's one happy girl," she said, nodding at the photograph of Ava staring wide-eyed at a birthday cake bristling with lit candles.

I turned the screen to her to give her a better look. "My daughter turned thirteen yesterday."

"They grow up fast, don't they?" she said.

"They do."

"I have a boy and a girl. The older one's starting university this fall."

"Wow," I said.

"Enjoy your drink."

"Thanks."

After she disappeared up the aisle, I turned to the window and stared dreamily out over the clouds. They were below us now, rolling mountains of white that looked dense enough to bounce you back up if you jumped off the wing.

At the end of that weekend in Madrid I was full of conflicting emotions. Thoughts of my brother were there again. In fact they hadn't really left me entirely, and now I wondered what game he was up to. I knew I was flying back into the heart of it, and most likely the game would involve me, even if he wasn't planning on collecting me at the airport in Toronto as he had thirteen months earlier. I'd heard from Monica only once after that first call, with no news of his whereabouts, and nothing had followed since.

I tried to sleep on the plane, but images of Saturday and Sunday night kept coming back to me—I'd stayed over at the old flat for a second evening after the party—and now the silly, sexy smile on Isabel's face kept spinning in my head. We'd made love those two nights with an intensity that rivaled the passion we'd felt when we were first together, and after we came we both started to laugh. It was something we used to do together but hadn't done in years. There was nothing in our period of separation that couldn't be let go of. Wasn't our capacity for atonement and absolution a measure of our best selves? That's what I thought the night after Ava's birthday as we lay together, those spasms still riding through our bodies.

I stared out the window and watched the clouds race by. Far below, the broad sheet of ocean went on and on, as if to the ends of the earth. I turned my camera back on and began swiping through the pictures again until I found the one that showed the three of us leaning over the birthday cake and smiling.

"Are you all right, sir? Sir? Are you okay?"

It was the flight attendant standing over me with a concerned smile on her face.

"Yes, sure. I'm fine. Thank you."

At customs I was interviewed by a large Caribbean woman who studied me a little longer than she should have. She tilted her head, squinting slightly.

For a moment I flashed back to the afternoon I'd been detained while trying to make that flight to Paris, and I might've squirmed. "Is there a problem?" I said.

"Where are you coming from, sir?" she said.

When I told her, she motioned to the eye. "Looks like you overstayed your welcome."

When I got home, just after six p.m., I called Isabel and told her I'd made it back all right. I grabbed a quick shower, turned on the TV and fixed myself a sandwich. It was already midnight Madrid time, but I'd been cooped up on that plane all day, and my head was still turning with everything that had happened.

I put my cycling gear on and biked down into the valley and burned up and down the trails, hoping to work off some nervous energy. After an hour I pulled up beside the sports field at the bottom of the Riverdale Park and watched a girls' soccer team take turns piggybacking partners up and down the hill. The coach, a short man in a blue tracksuit, circulated among his players, egging them on with encouraging shouts. Overhead the gulls were gulping down dragonflies as they swarmed by the thousands, three or four dozen birds taking turns cutting through the shimmering mist of wings, snapping and choking them down. I walked my bike up the hill and watched as the last insects were picked off and the gulls flew back toward the lake.

The new fall term started the day after tomorrow. In Madrid the term kicked off in October, but here the end of summer came earlier. This was a season I loved from my old school days, remembering the heady sense that another great adventure was finally beginning. In the air and the light over the valley that afternoon I felt and saw hints of the change of seasons and tried to slow them down and hold them in my mind and my heart. Here was my last autumn in this city, and I wasn't saddened to know I would soon be leaving. The moment carried such weight and significance that I lingered there minutes longer than I might have otherwise. And as I turned to leave it occurred to me for the first time since that phone call three days ago that my brother might actually be in trouble. I started for his house, hoping for a sign. He'd be back by now, I thought, of course he would.

I saw three police cars parked in front when I

turned onto his street a few minutes later. A dozen or so people were gathered on the sidewalk. At the front door a yellow police cordon barred access to the house, and a police officer stood there flipping through a small notepad. I dropped my bike and stepped forward and identified myself. The officer pivoted inside and called down the hallway. Then a detective appeared and questioned me as to the whereabouts of my brother. When I asked what this was all about, he told me that Kaj Adolfsson was dead.

✷| Epilogue

A strange portrait of my brother
was rolled out before the public eye in the days and
weeks that followed. At first I rejected the profile of a
man who had more time for sailing and partying than
he did for his family. It was too ugly, and too true.
Cable news showed photographs of him. In one, his
arm was draped over the shoulder of a well-known ath-
lete, cigars alight; in another he was hoisting a glass of
champagne at a New Year's Eve party. The photos only
added weight to the argument that he'd led a frivolous
life. There was a nod to the inevitability of the whole
sad mess.

To drive the point home, the spokesman for the
Adolfsson family—a man named Edvard, who'd flown
in on receiving word of his brother-in-law's death—
spoke movingly to a local reporter about Kaj's gentle
nature and sense of goodwill. I watched all this with
grotesque fascination. Of course Monica didn't subject
herself to any such interviews. On the late news one evening Hilary and I saw the *Get My Kicks*, Nate's sailboat,
moored in the Naples harbor, along with a catalogue
of the places he'd supposedly visited before coming
north. We learned from those reports that my brother
had checked out of the Cove Inn on Monday morning

and was driven by cab to the Naples Municipal Airport and then flew to Tampa International, where he caught his flight home. The airport limo service he frequently used was waiting for him that afternoon. The driver, who recognized this frequent customer, described his demeanor as nervous and agitated, "like a man late for something big that's going to happen." But he thought nothing of it, really, he said into the camera. He got fares like that all the time. Likewise, he didn't think it strange that a man—Kaj Adolfsson, obviously—seemed to be waiting for his passenger on the front steps of that big house on Riverdale Avenue. In a statement that might have seemed remarkable only to me, the driver said that he supposed this "was the guy's brother, the brother of the accused." I don't know why he would have said that, for Kaj and I looked nothing alike. In other words, though, there was nothing unusual at all about the scene. The driver helped the client with his bag and, after collecting his fare, drove off as the real drama unfolded.

Monica was already upstairs going through the boys' closets by this time. Titus and Quinn were out back saying good-bye to their tree fort. Nate, who surely would've been surprised to see his wife's boyfriend standing on his doorstep, pushed past him and headed for the stairs, Kaj following behind. After hearing the story my brother told to me in the weeks that followed, I wondered what Kaj had been thinking as he stood outside watching the neighborhood while waiting for his girlfriend to clear out some things from her former home. Part of me wanted to believe he was contemplating how sadly spouses sometimes end things between themselves, sneaking around through each other's lives—in effect turning against those they once loved. Another part wanted to think that he'd drawn the line there, deciding that this simply wasn't who he was, a man who pushes himself into another man's home. He had won fair and square but would afford that fundamental respect to my brother. He couldn't understand the full scope of the story, of course, or who my brother really was. At least I doubt that Monica would have told him everything, and he knew nothing about the girl I'd caught Nate with. He would've known only that a marriage had ended, and he'd come out on top where the two men were concerned. Until the moment Nate grabbed the putter while storming through the house, it had been a fair fight, just a matter of rivals in love.

Maybe it had been lying on the couch. Or leaning against a wall. I'd seen it in various places. He was a man for whom leisure, good times and easy distractions always needed to be close at hand. So there it was, the putter—snatched up and steadying him as he took the stairs two at a time to find his wife in the final stages of clearing his sons out of his life. The boys were in the backyard when it happened. All it took was thirty seconds, maybe a minute. They didn't see or hear a thing as their father bludgeoned the Swede to death, then dropped the golf club and walked back into the late afternoon.

. . .

But why did he come back in the first place? In the end, he said, it came down to courage. He'd failed himself so often—and he told me this three weeks later in the Don Jail, where he'd been sent to wait for his trial—that he'd simply been unable to do what he knew he should've done, which was to leave and start an entirely new life. Everything would have found its proper place if he'd managed to disappear into a wide and waiting America as he'd intended. That's all he needed to do. But he didn't feel like a new man as he'd set out on the journey of his lifetime. He was not reborn. Without the limits he'd always known— the safety of a family, first of a mother and father, of a brother and a kindly uncle, and then of a wife and, finally, children—the freedom he'd longed for didn't taste as great as he'd thought it would. There had always been something to return to. Wasn't that the greatest irony, that what you need to leave behind are things you're unable to abandon? What he found waiting for him out there was solitude, and that wasn't something he'd prepared himself for. He couldn't oper-ate like that. It just wasn't in his DNA. It took him less than two days to see that.

I watched his eyes as this story unfolded. He was sitting behind a sheet of Plexiglas in the visitors' meeting room, leaning on both elbows and holding a phone against his ear. I was on the other side. His voice was tinny and distant, though if that plastic barrier hadn't separated us I could have touched the hairs on his head.

"You ride that bike of yours over here?" he said. "You're always on that stupid thing."

"It's chained up outside. A lot of thieves in the neighborhood, I hear."

He smiled, then resumed his story.

He walked the streets of Naples with a sinking heart. It was like he'd forgotten about the plan entirely. None of it made sense to him anymore. All the world lay before him, and here he was with no idea what to do with it. That's what fantasies turn into, he said—a stifling reality shot through with regret. It was the final truth of the matter that stopped him, and this was that he couldn't leave. He didn't have what it took to snap his fingers and disappear. He just wasn't like that, he said, leaning forward and tapping the glass with the phone, then putting it back up against his ear. "You know, wandering around Naples, I didn't even remember what I was doing there. I couldn't figure out why I wasn't beside myself with joy. I was free, right? I'd been dreaming of it for years. We all do. You get pushed far enough, that's what everyone does."

"Some people," I said.

"And that's when it came to me. I was standing on that wharf that juts out into the sea with Mexico on the horizon and my freedom in every direction. And that's when I saw the difference between me and you. I couldn't just disappear like you did. Because I'm not like you."

He was trying to punish me, I decided. Much like he'd tried to punish me by taking Riley into his bed. But I still didn't understand why at this grim stage of his life he so desperately needed to hold sway over me.

Titus and Quinn were doing as well as could be expected. I didn't try to confront the issue with Titus that his dad had beaten a man's brains out with a golf club. What had happened was too big, too confusing, to digest. In mid-November I took them to Disney World in Florida, calling it an early Christmas present. I knew they needed to get out of school and out of Toronto altogether, so I shepherded them onto a plane, and down into the warm weather we flew. Just the smell of the air seemed to have an effect for a time. We tripped down Gang Plank Falls and did the Surf Pool and Shark Reef in Typhoon Lagoon. I thought that at least for a while they'd be able to forget about what was going on in their lives. Then two days later, while we were driving out to Cape Canaveral to tour the Astronaut Hall of Fame, Titus turned to me and said, "I won't blame you when the time comes."

Not sure what he was talking about, I said, "You can explain that one if you like."

"The trial."

"I don't know if I'll be called," I said.

"Oh, you'll be called."

"I doubt your dad wants to hear what I have to say on the matter of character."

"Don't sugarcoat it if you are," he said.

"I guess I wouldn't."

"Just remember what he did," he said, then turned and looked at his little brother asleep in the backseat. "Quinn still thinks it was just a fight. And Kaj's just gone off on some trip or something."

The Florida landscape rolled by, billboards and windblown plastic bags hanging like laundry in the branches of the swamp chestnuts along the highway.

Looking over at Titus, I saw that he was now the very picture of his father. The strong chin and high, handsome cheekbones. His long hair hung partly over his eyes. I'd noticed in the past few weeks that his voice had started to crack.

"You're stronger than your dad," I told him. "I know what you're thinking."

He was staring out the window. He didn't look at me or say anything.

"You're not going to be like him, Titus."

He flicked the hair out of his eyes with a sharp turn of his head. "You sound pretty sure of that," he said.

"I know it better than I know anything."

He believed he'd been given a look into his future, or part of it, and what he saw disturbed him.

But my brother's character was not his son's fate. The thoughtfulness and the silences that fell over Titus were the opposite of the ravenous hunger for acceptance I'd seen lurch to life in Nate after our parents died. Through to the end of our vacation Titus carried that worry on his face and in his heart. Out of the corner of my eye I'd catch him staring off at nothing or standing there with his hands in his front pockets looking down at his shoes. I knew what he was doing. He was struggling with it, as we all were. But he was more alive to the possibility of his own failure than anyone I'd ever met. Still some part of him was aware of this—maybe something as basic as a conscience—and so he would fight that much harder to find the good in the world, I was convinced. I tried to help him see this in himself.

Along with their mother, the boys had been in counseling for a month or so now, trying to put their lives back together. I could tell it was uncomfortable living in Kaj's house, for all the obvious reasons, but they would not be staying long in any case. Once the house in Riverdale sold, Monica planned to buy a new one in the west end, as far from either of those neighborhoods as you could get without leaving the city.

I'd biked down a few times and seen that the Realtor's sign was up now, the black-and-red placard staked in the grass and swinging poignantly in the autumn wind, a sad reminder of how dreams can go so far off the rails.

Around this time Hilary came to the house to celebrate over a bottle of wine. She'd sent off her collection of essays to a university press down in the States that day, to be admired or ignored, she didn't yet know. But she was feeling good that the project was finally off her desk. We were only friends now. I'd told her about my plans to return to Madrid and that Isabel and I might give it another shot. This news didn't surprise her. I suspect she believed something in me had been shaken to the core in the aftermath of the murder and that I needed to mend fences with those closest to me.

After supper we turned on the news and heard that a typhoon had torn through the Philippines at Luzon. I didn't make the connection at first, but this was where she'd worked with that NGO years before. Three villages had disappeared. The images were incredible— corrugated-iron roofs and crumbled shacks, toothpick trees, toy cars, a whole landscape swept under a world of mud. She immediately scoured the Internet for details, and over the next few days she got in touch with some old associates in Manila and hatched a plan to go back again to help. Two weeks later, as I drove her out to the airport, I said how happy I was for her. She'd been spinning her wheels here, anyway, and now she was going where she needed to be. "Sometimes good things come out of the worst sort of disaster," I said. "Maybe that's a terrible thing to say, but it's true."

"It's been a good year," she said.

I nodded, still driving.

"I don't know if you ever heard me say that."

"It's been a good year for me, too," I said.

That wasn't exactly true, not in any comprehensive sense, but it was where Hilary was concerned. Miles and Holly had both slipped back into the past, where they belonged, and now Hilary was moving off to a life that she hadn't invited me into and that held no interest for me.

Did Holly ever know that her daughter had given herself to my brother just days before he committed that second, greater crime? I never knew. But as she might have turned the earth in her garden that fall, she may well have wondered if this recent family history didn't connect back to the night the three of us were together for the last time in Montreal. Did she wonder about the man Miles would've become, the life he would've led? Where would the three of us be had the course of events taken a less dramatic turn? And in a moment of whimsy, I imagined an annual get-together on some sun-scorched Greek island where we ate and drank like in the old days and did our level best to invoke better times. But she was gone, a ghost in my life now, swept away like those villages in the far-off Philippines, and all I could do was hope and remember her as the girl she used to be.

That afternoon, after dropping Hilary at the airport, I detoured to a cemetery I hadn't visited in more than twenty years. It was the tail end of a cold sunny day, and I'd been pondering the question Isabel had posed that night she held the ice against my face three months earlier. What should I have done in my time here that I'd failed to do? It was almost dark when I found the headstone, and as I stood by Miles's grave I told him something about the man I'd become, my successes and failures, about the woman I'd married and had a daughter with and that I hoped he was at peace and somehow, maybe looking down on us now, knew that I had not betrayed him.

. . .

It was a long hard fall and early winter. I had the academy to keep me busy, and once or twice a week I called
Madrid and spoke with Ava and Isabel, counting down
the days to my departure. I visited Nate regularly,
though we had little to say to each other. I was all he
had left. The trial date had finally been set, and the
three lawyers he had working for him had decided that
I should be called as a character witness. I was to tell
the world, in my own words, what sort of a man my
brother was.

He put his hand on the Plexiglas and said, "You
know me better than anyone else does."

I met his hand with mine, fingers and palms separated by the cold plastic, and said I would do what I
could, though the truth was I didn't feel I knew him
at all anymore.

"That's all I can ask," he said.

I flew to Spain the next day. I tried to sleep on the
plane but couldn't. I watched two movies, read some
magazines, and finally the turbulent coastline of Por-
tugal appeared outside my window. Forty-five minutes later, when we banked over Madrid, I was able to
identify the Plaza Mayor, the Retiro Park, even Atocha
Street, or what I thought was Atocha Street, where Isabel and I spent time in the back of a police car before
going home together.

Once I cleared customs and immigration, I took a
cab to the Reina Victoria, thinking it best, at least for

now, to give Isabel and myself time to adjust to the new possibilities that had arisen between us.

The cleaning lady was still working on the room I usually stayed in, so I sipped coffee in the bar downstairs until a bellhop walked over and told me my room was ready. I got cleaned up, unpacked and ate a proper breakfast, then went into work.

It was the last day before the Christmas break, and the academy was buzzing. Rosa welcomed me back as she always did, with two pecks on the cheek. I told her she smelled like a pine forest.

She smiled and pointed at the Christmas tree she'd set up in the corner. "Always working," she said.

I walked through the academy wishing my students and teachers a happy holiday. The stack of bonus checks was waiting for me on my desk. I put on a silly white beard Rosa had purchased for the occasion and handed out the envelopes.

At the end of the day I crossed back over the street and looked in the window of the café. It was packed with students and starry-eyed lovers and Christmas shoppers stopping in to warm themselves over a hot drink. I watched an old man and a little girl rolling a blue marble back and forth between cups of steaming chocolate. They were sitting at the table closest to the window, and at the next table over were two tired-looking backpackers conferring over a copy of *The Rough Guide to Spain*. Then Ava called me on my cell and said, "I can't wait to see you. We're already here."

"I'm on my way. I'll be there in twenty minutes."

"Dad?"

"Yes, sweetheart?"

"I've got the best one ever. You'll never get this one. Not in a million years."

"I'm shaking in my boots," I said.

"It's worse than tough. This one'll twist your brain into a pretzel. *Worse* than a pretzel."

"Let's have it," I said.

"Now?"

"I'll need a head start, right?"

"But you've got to promise me something."

"What's that?" I said.

"There's no giving up this time. Deal?"

"Deal," I said.

And then she told me her latest brainteaser. Long and complicated, it worked on a number of levels. She made me repeat it back to her to make sure I had it straight.

"All right," she said. "Have fun with that one."

After we hung up I looked into the café a short while longer and started pondering my daughter's new riddle. The backpackers were hoisting their heavy bags, getting set to move on, but the old man was still sitting there with the girl. It looked like they were in no hurry to leave, rolling that marble back and forth over the white tabletop and sipping at their chocolate.

I started walking toward the restaurant where my wife and daughter were waiting, my jacket open in the cold winter air. All the cafés and sidewalks were busy with people loaded down with bags of Christmas gifts. It was a wonderful time of the year to find yourself in a city like Madrid. The storefront windows flooded the street with a warm glow. The taverns and restaurants were filling up. The smell of chestnuts and roasting chicken carried on the air. Briefcase in hand, I admired the lights and the beauty in the faces of the people I passed while trying to solve my daughter's riddle. But the longer I thought about it, the more confusing it became. Every time I believed I was closing in on the answer, a fresh and richer likelihood presented itself to me, and then this one, too, would soon find itself stripped away by an even newer and more exciting probability. And finally, twenty blocks later, pushing through the door of our old favorite restaurant, I saw my daughter sitting beside her mother, and the smile that grew on Ava's face when our eyes met made it clear to me that the possibilities were practically endless.

ACKNOWLEDGMENTS

The author wishes to acknowledge the support of
the Toronto Arts Council, the Ontario Arts Council
and the Canada Council, as well as the kind folks
at the Little Inn of Bayfield, Ontario.

A NOTE ON THE TYPE

This book was set in Adobe Garamond. Designed for the
Adobe Corporation by Robert Slimbach, the fonts are based
on types first cut by Claude Garamond (c. 1480–1561).
Garamond was a pupil of Geoffroy Tory's and is believed to
have followed the Venetian models, although he introduced a
number of important differences, and it is to him that we owe
the letter we now know as "old style." He gave to his letters
a certain elegance and feeling of movement that won their
creator an immediate reputation and the patronage
of Francis I of France.

Typeset by Scribe,
Philadelphia, Pennsylvania

Printed and bound by Berryville Graphics,
Berryville, Virginia

Designed by Robert C. Olsson